Bay Bizzness
San Francisco Oakland Richmond Vallejo
The Anthology

Table of Contents

By
Khatari Lyrics Brown
Caleigh Blue Danae Braggs

Oakland

By
Author Khatari

SYNOPSIS

T he city of Oakland has been known for many things throughout its history; unfortunately, the notoriety of its gangs, drugs, violence, mayhem, and murder has long overshadowed its true beauty and history. From the Black Panthers to drug-dealing gangstas, the streets of Oakland changed drastically. Can it be corrected, or are they destined to live in hell on earth?

Ty Dollar-Sign is the leader of one of Oakland's most dangerous and violent gangs to date, The Gas Nation. He and his crew of Killah's are on a crash course of making their legendary imprint on the streets of Oakland in the worst way.

A phone call from Ty's dying father will reveal shocking truths that will make Ty re-evaluate not only himself but the path he is traveling.

Find out if the hidden truths and a forgotten legacy are enough to change his course. Or is he destined to crash and burn?

CHAPTER 1

(2003 Oakland, California)

The sound of the Luniz's new hit song Oakland Raiders blasted from the speakers of my 1988 Buick Grand National GNX. I stood outside of my whip as fitted as a nigga could be. I had a pair of black, Red Monkey jeans and a pair of Nike Air Max. The purple Bathing Ape hoodie that I was rock'n matched the Candy Grape paint on my Grand National.

I was parked in the McDonald's parking lot on 98th and E. 14th Street. They changed the name from East 14th to International Blvd. But to niggaz from Oakland, a.k.a. "The Town" this street will forever be the infamous E-1-4 (ee-one-foe). This was the strip, and tonight the strip was poppin!

There are at least three to four hundred mothafuckas out on the strip tonight. It's a Sideshow and this mothafucka is on and poppin! In the intersection, niggaz were taking turns hitting donuts and figure eight'n everything from Chevy Camaro's and Nova's to Mustangs and Cutlasses. The smell of burnt rubber was heavy in the air as tires spun rapidly against the hard pavement burning the rubber off the tires.

A Sideshow was virtually a hood car show. Niggaz came from all over the city to showcase their whips. All the niggaz with high performance and supped-up shit under the hoods would come flying up the block. They would be swinging donuts and figure eight'n in the middle of the street or doing burnouts. Then you had niggaz that brought their shit out to stunt and showcase how clean and expensive their shit was. This was the category I fell under cause my shit was on point. You even had niggaz that came out in clean whips, but they were there just to let mothafuckas hear the sound system they had in their shit.

This is how life is in East Oakland. Fast money, fast cars, and fast women. Town Bizness!

I'm a full fledge Town representative, straight the fuck up! My name is Tyrone Johnson, a.k.a. Ty Dollar-Sign, leader of The Gas Nation. Word on the street is we are the coldest and most dangerous crew to ever come out of Oakland. But I'm not here to try to make myself look good. I'll let the storytellers handle that. I'ma just-do me.

I was in the middle of rolling a blunt filled with that Grand-Daddy Purple Kush when she walked up. Even though I was concentrating on what I was doing, a nigga had to stay on point out here. So, my antennas were up.

"Damn, Ty, no matter where we at or how many niggaz are around, you always trying to outshine a niggaz." I didn't bother responding. I just continued rolling my blunt.

The wind carried the smell of her perfume to my nose. I didn't know what it was because I had never smelled it before, but damn, that shit was fire.

"I know you're not going to sit there and ignore me, Ty. I could have any one of these niggaz out here tonight. Yet I chose to walk over here and give you some time, and you just gonna sit there and ignore me like I'm some random ass hood-rat out here gold-digging or something?" Her little attitude was sexy as fuck.

I finally lifted my head so I could look at her. Her name was Laurice Fleming, and she was by far one of the most, if not the baddest chicks in Oakland. Her face was beautiful, and her skin was a flawless deep mocha that a niggaz eyes could drink in all day. She was 5'1" and probably weighed about 210 lbs. All ass, thighs, and tits. I'm talking the kind of body that the nigga Rick James was talking about when he made that record Brick House.

I let my eyes travel slowly up her gorgeous body while licking my blunt, like I was licking up her shapely legs, looking for something a little sweeter. My eyes continued over her flat stomach and D-cup breast until they found her best attribute. Her deep hazel eyes were sexy as hell.

"That's the problem right there, Laurice. I didn't ask you to walk over here, nor did I ask you for any of your time. So, what makes you think I owe you some attention?" I know she could see the spark of humor in my eyes. If not, the way my tongue slid across the blunt told her that I was fucking with her.

"Boy, please! You sitting there licking that blunt like you wanna give a bitch a whole lot more than just your attention; so why don't you stop fronting." She put her hand on her hips and leaned back on her heels. Making that ass pop out. That mothafucka was like a giant kickball.

I was about to respond to Laurice when the crowds' noise and energy became frantic, like something was wrong. I looked for the cause of the hype. On the corner, the nigga Manny (everyone knew Manny and his brother George because they were regulars at the Sideshows) was swinging his black on-black seven-deuce Cutlass. As they skidded across the paved street, his tires made an ugly screeching sound. Just that fast, the crowd jumped off the Richter scale. Manny had the best handles in Oakland. That nigga could be flying down the street doing like 50 miles per hour, lock his tires up and start swang'n his shit. Niggaz have tried to copy Manny only to crash their shit.

Manny had his windows rolled down and somehow had popped the trunk. Leave it up to that nigga to put an automatic trunk release on an old school. Suddenly Keak-Da-Sneak's new song *Hyphy* (hi-fee) *Remix* came on. Mothafuckas lost their minds. Everybody started getting Hyphy. Bodies were jerking every which way but loose. Dreadlocks swayed and flew in the air as if they were dancing on top of people's heads themselves.

The best way to describe Hyphy is its organized chaos. At first glance, it looked as if mothafuckas were jumping, twisting, and jerking out of control. But a closer look would reveal that every jerk, every move, was, choreographed and timed precisely to the beat of the music.

It was the newest form of dancing that had just hit the Bay Area, and it hit hard. Hyphy was a way of life, and we were living it. Fun and free. "Oh shit, Ty! Look at these mothafuckas! They're about to do some crazy shit!" Laurice called out excitedly.

I looked back toward the corner, and Manny's Cutlass had come to a complete stop facing another vehicle. His little brother George had pulled up in his Canary yellow Camaro. That bitch was hot as Hell. The cars were a few feet apart, and then Manny hit the gas a couple of seconds before George. Before I knew it, both cars whipped into a donut going opposite directions. At the height of the donut, the vehicles would sort of drift before hitting a donut in the opposite direction. The result was the cars would swing in the formation of an eight. That's what we called figure-eight'n. Manny and his brother were both figure-eight'n at the same time in opposite directions. It was the cleanest shit I have ever seen two niggaz do in their cars. "Ty, do you remember that time I begged you to hit a donut while we were in your Malibu?" It was hard hearing her over all the noise.

A fight broke out across the parking lot and the crowd got even louder. As I watched, I took a moment to light my blunt. I took a long drag on my blunt and stood up. The Kush threatening a niggaz lungs. I let the smoke roll out from my nostrils like a young vet. Laurice looked at me hungrily, with lust-filled eyes, as I stepped to her and wrapped my arm around her waist.

I pulled her body as close to mine as I could. Her soft breast smacked against my chest. My hardness let her know I remembered that day very well. "You remember how tight you held a nigga while I was swang'n that bitch?"

She smiled and bit down on her bottom lip. I became excited in response to her grinding her pelvis into me.

"Hmmm.... I seem to remember more vividly how good it felt..."

She never got a chance to finish. The fight on the other side of the parking lot reached an apex when someone started shooting. I pulled

Laurice down with me when I crouched down. I instantly dropped the blunt I was holding and snatched my chrome .45 off my hip.

Even though that shit didn't have anything to do with us, I ducked down behind my National because everybody knows a bullet has no name. More importantly, most mothafuckas can't shoot which is why you never know who's going to be on the receiving end.

"Niggaz always gotta fuck some shit up!" I managed to hear her say over the noise and chaos.

Instead of responding, I rushed her into the car. She had to climb over the driver's seat. This gave me an excellent view of that phat ass of hers. I couldn't concentrate on it long. Some dumb ass nigga was trynna knock me out of the way and jack me for my shit. I half spun around, giving me room to bring the .45 up to his head. The niggaz head snapped back like somebody knocked him in his shit with a Louisville Slugger. In reality, the force of the big ass slug from my .45 did it. A cloud of shit blew out of the back of his head. Was he stupid? Trynna take my shit.

I didn't waste any time jumping inside the car and getting the fuck out of there. Grabbing a room with Laurice for the night sounded a whole lot better to me than getting locked up and spending the night and most likely longer in North County Jail.

As I weaved in and out of traffic, I didn't give one thought to the dead mothafucka who tried to carjack me. All my thoughts were on Laurice and all the freaky shit we were about to do. That nigga made his choice, and I made mine.

CHAPTER 2

Last night was beyond wild; it was fucking out of this world! We were at it until the wee hours of the morning. If I remember correctly, we went four or five rounds. Shit, it could've been six. All I can say for sure is if the cameras would've been rolling last night, we would've made the hottest porn movie in the world. Hell, I would've stayed another night if it hadn't been for the phone call I got from my Pops. He told me that he needed to see me right away. Said it was an emergency. Pop's ain't never said those words to me.

I bought Laurice some breakfast before dropping her off. Then I made my way over to West Oakland to see what the old man thought was so urgent. The moment I stepped through the door, a strange feeling came over me that I didn't understand. I found the old man seated at the dining room table in the dark. He didn't even notice when I walked into the room. He just sat there with a blank look on his face.

I noticed his clothes were wrinkled, and he looked like he hadn't groomed himself in several days. I sat down in a chair across from him. As I did, I noticed a bottle of bourbon sitting on the kitchen counter. There was an empty glass in front of him. I studied his face for a moment. Somehow, he looked like he had aged since I'd last seen him, and the old man's hair wasn't combed. Stress lines had formed on his forehead. His eyes looked at me, but his stare was a thousand miles beyond me.

My heart became heavy instantly because I had never seen him this way. I was always used to Pop being strong and assertive. Yet he looked bothered, shit, even scared.

"Pop, what's up?" My voice was filled with concern. When he didn't answer me, I leaned forward and smacked my hand against the table. "Pop!" My voice was louder this time. Stern.

The glass that was in front of him rattled, and it got his attention. He blinked and looked genuinely surprised to see me sitting before him.

"T-Ty-Tyrone, son, you've made it." His voice sounded hoarse like he'd been crying, and it was weak.... low.

"Of course, I made it, you said it was an emergency, so I came. Why you sitting here all in the dark? And why your hair and clothes look like shit Pops? What's going on?"

"Got some heavy shit I gotta drop in yo lap, son. But first, go in that kitchen and grab that bottle of Yack."

"Some heavy shit like what, Pop?" I asked him.

"Boy, go in there and do what I told you to do. Questioning me like you crazy or something." For a brief moment, he appeared focused, and I saw my Pops. Not the broken down, worried old man that I saw when I walked in, but the rugged hardened man I've always known. The stubborn fool that spoke like an army general.

I got up and did as the old man said. I grabbed myself a glass before walking back to the table. I sat the bottle down in front of him, and then I sat down. This was his show, so I figured I'd let him run it however he saw fit. Pop poured the both of us a half glass of bourbon. He picked up his glass and drained about half of its contents. I was still waiting on him to talk, so I just sat there. Pops had one of them old-school grandfather clocks hanging in the living room; I could softly hear the ticking of the second hand as it ticked away.

Pops licked his lips after taking that first swallow and stared blankly at the glass. If the bottle wasn't halfway gone already, I would've thought that drink was his first time tasting it. He smacked his lips. Then told me the worst news that I could never be prepared to hear.

"Tyrone, I'm dying, son." He didn't even look at me. He just said that shit, a matter of fact like, with no emotion.

What the fuck was I supposed to say to that?

My Pops wasn't the type to play games, especially about some shit like this, so I knew he was serious. What didn't I know was how in the fuck a nigga was supposed to respond to some shit like that. What the fuck did he expect me to say? Pops and I didn't have the best relationship. I mean, we had a cool bond, but while he was in prison, the streets were my daddy. I was grown by the time he came home, so we sort of started from there. The bond was more like he was just one of the O.G.'s I fucked with and had some love for, more than it was a bond between father and son.

I finally managed the only thing I could get out. "What's wrong?" I picked up my glass and downed that shit.

"Stage three colon cancer; doc says he don't know how I've managed to go so long without having any symptoms or experiencing severe complications. Said there's nothing that can be done. Cancer managed to spread throughout my body to other organs and shit." He reached for the bottle and refilled both our glasses. This time he damn near filled them to the top. He sat the bottle down on the table and looked at me for the first time. "Doc says I only got a few months left."

I picked up my glass and took another long swallow. As the smooth bourbon slid down my throat, a hot lone tear shot its way down my cheek. This was still my mothafucking father. We might not have been super mothafucking close, but we were cool! And we were getting tighter every fucking day. Why in the fuck would God fuck with that?

My body was starting to get hot. I knew it was from the bourbon, but I told myself it was because of the news. "Damn Pop. That's some fucked up shit for a nigga to have to hear. I know it'll be dumb ass fuck to ask you if you're alright because nobody can be alright after hearing something like this. Is there anything you need me to do? Whatever it is, just say it and it's done." I tried to show strength. I had to be strong so he could be strong.

He smiled a saddened smile. The old man looked like he weighted the world on his shoulders. Pops was six-foot-four, two hundred and sixty-plus pounds. He was a man's man in every sense of the phrase. But he didn't look it sitting across the table from me. Though I could tell he was doing his best to stay strong and remain "G". His sloped shoulders, wrinkled face and the saddened lost look in his eyes told a different story. They spoke of a man who was desperately trying to hold on. My Pops is now a man on the verge of breaking, a man who is too stubborn to quit yet too weak physically to continue. It hurt my heart that for the first time, I saw fear on my Pop's face.

"You know son, I've been through a lot of shit. Seen a lot of shit and believe me, I've done a lot of shit. So, I really can't cry or complain about much. Death is something we all must face one day. Some sooner than others, but eventually we all must go and stand before that bitch. I'm just glad that I got the opportunity to come home and become a part of your life. Get to know you and my grandson before my clock ran out of time." He looked up at me and an identical tear was rolling down his cheek. "Ty, the only thing I need from you son is the one thing I can't get more of and that's time. I need you to spend some time with me. I have a story to tell you. It'll also tell you what really happened to me and hopefully prevent history from repeating itself."

From the look in his eyes, I could tell that this was important to him. Shit, I was willing and ready to attempt to bring the old nigga the Virgin Mary herself if he would have asked for her. All he wanted was for me to listen while he got some shit off of his chest. Hell yeah, I'd give him that.

"I got you Pop, I'm here for however long you need me to be. Whatever it is just say the word."

"Alright. First, we're going to need another bottle. It's one in that cabinet over the sink; go grab that before we get started." He was refilling his glass as he spoke.

One thing about the men in our family is we could put away a nice amount of alcohol without losing our shit. We weren't the type to get drunk. We just loved to drink.

I grabbed the other bottle and sat back down at the table. I picked my glass back up and took a drink, more so out of the need to do something than wanting a sip.

"Now hopefully this little story I'm bout to tell you will shed some truth about the city of Oakland and us as black men. Who knows maybe.... just maybe it'll inspire you to become a better father than I ever was." Pops cleared his throat. I'm not too sure but I swear it looked like he wanted to cry.

In all the years I've known him, I've never seen or heard of Joseph Taylor crying. He's always been tough—the sort of guy that would chew on nails and crap out fire. I didn't want to embarrass him, so I turned my head.

I heard him take a couple of deep breaths. He cleared his throat and spoke. "I'ma take you back to a time before there were gangs in Oakland. Back to the time when black men still had pride in themselves and self-respect..."

I sat and listened as Pops took me on a trip down memory lane to see the streets from a perspective, I'd never seen before.

He began talkin...

CHAPTER 3

(Pops is talking...)

Back in the '60s and '70s, even at the beginning of the '80s, Oakland, California, was a city filled with hardworking people. Blacks, for the most part, were predominately in West Oakland. It's hard to believe today, but East Oakland was considered to be an inner-city suburb. All the Streets were lined with Oak trees. On both sides of each street throughout the entire neighborhood, a person would find miles and miles of Oak trees. In fact, it's how the city got its name Oakland because it was the land of the Oak Tree.

To most of its residents, Oakland, California was truly our Black Mecca. When the Black Panther Party for Self Defense decide to make West Oakland the location of its headquarters, it gave the lower class, hardworking black man, a sense of pride, dignity, and a sense of belonging. Philadelphia may be the city of brotherly love, but I'm telling you Oakland, California sure had a lot of brotherly love itself.

Of course, all of that was before Felix Mitchell and the 69 Mob took over. Although Big Fee (Felix was sometimes referred to as Big Fee or Felix the Cat after the cartoon character) and his organization were not single-handedly responsible for the demise of Oakland. Anyone who has the heart to do so will say that Big Fee and the 69 Mob gave the proverbial push that began the onslaught. Felix Mitchell invented the machine, which was a well-run and methodically thinking organization that sells drugs in an organized way. Metaphorically speaking with the 69 Mob, Big Fee ran his drug empire much like a Fortune 500 company.

Other machines (most would call them gangs) that followed continued the wave of drugs, violence, and mayhem that began with the 69 Mob.

The drugs and violence had replaced the love and dignity the city once thrived on. Streets that were once lined with beautiful Oaks were now littered with broken down abandoned cars, used and broken needles, and crack pipes. The gutters are polluted with used condoms and every other form of sick and vile shit a person could think of. Liquor stores crowd corners that once housed YMCA's and boxing gyms. Once new and well-kept apartments are now run down and rodent infested. Prostitutes fill the stairways, performing tricks for just enough chump change to pay for their next fix. Sistahs who once had too much pride, self-worth, and self-respect, are now in darkened stairways on their knees.

Well.... That was... until today!

Today is the day the Revolutionary Guerilla will snatch the streets out of the vile clutches of the drug dealers, pimps, gang bangers, and so-called Mack's or Boss Playas.

It's the summer of 1993 and I'm on my way home from a six-year sentence for a double drug conviction. Good behavior got me released after actually doing a little more than three years. Some of the most reflective time of a man's life is done behind the cold steel bars of a prison cell. Yet I must admit that as I travel along on this Greyhound bus, sitting behind the chick whose baby doesn't believe in the concept of peace, my mind can't help but reflect on life and all the times that have led to me sitting on this bus with a plastic garbage bag that contains what little material possessions I had left.

Across the aisle and one seat back, a young brotha was listening to a walkman and rapping along with the song like he was the only mothafucka on the bus. Two seats in front of him a black couple was arguing. Even with all of this going on, I had my head tilted back and my eyes closed with a smile on my face.

While I was in prison, I saw so much death and witnessed so much betrayal, I gave up on believing in people. I thank God that I not only survived but I was fortunate enough to make it out of them walls. Why? Because I knew like many others that once you entered the concrete and bobbed wire walls of prison, there was no guarantee you would ever make it back out.

Before going to prison I was a young, wild, money-hungry Cat. Just like every other young black kid in the ghetto. I held dreams of fast money, fast cars, and fast women. I jumped in the game ten toes down looking for my pot of gold at the end of the rainbow. I had a nice little run too. Looking back on it now, I had to admit to myself that I used to be part of the problem. While in prison I met The Brotha's and became educated on social justice and true economics. I learned ideologies like Democratic Centralism, Scientific Socialism, and Revolutionary Nationalism. I learned about brothas like Frederick Douglass, Marcus Garvey, Chancellor Williams, and many others.

Being from Oakland I knew all about The Black Panther Party. But in prison, I was able to learn what The Black Panther Party really wahat the movement was about. The more I learned, the more I wanted. I wanted to know more, wanted to actually do morer the first time in my life I wanted to be more.

As time went on, I was beginning to feel ashamed of who I used to be. I didn't realize how ignorant and foolish I was out there in the streets selling poison to my people—destroying my community. The Brotha's provided me with the information and education I needed in oforto learn what a real black man was.

A little after a year into my prison sentence, I took an oath and swore my dying allegiance to the organization and became one of the Brotha's. Once I took my oath, my teachings multiplied—my opinion of self-changed. My entire view of life was forever altered. I was preparing myself mentally, physically, and psychologically to take up arms in a war. San Quentin State Prison had been my boot camp and home of my basic training. Now I was being deployed to the battlefield. I was going to war.

I could see the West Oakland Greyhound Station from the freeway as the bus was exiting. Everybody on the bus restlessly moved around. Some were excited to finally be reaching their destination while others were just happy to have a momentary break in their long uneventful trip.

It was still early morning as the bus turned onto San Pablo getting ready to round the corner and pull into the back of the station where the buses go. Already, even in the early morning, people filled the streets. Brotha's were spread along the street with their boom boxes blasting. Their clothes were multicolored and baggy. I had heard about a new style called Cross Colors that had come out not too long ago, but I had never actually seen it. Even the Sistahs were dressed in bright-colored baggy clothes. They were all on the sidewalk talking, laughing, and having a good time. There were a few hustlers in the midst as well. I could easily spot them because no matter what they were doing, they would nervously glance around every so often. Not to mention all the hustlers usually wore oversized puff coats to conceal whatever form of weapon they were carrying to protect themselves—usually a gun.

When I stepped off the bus, I took a big deep breath. There was nothing at all like that good ole Bay Area air! I can't describe it, but that Bay air had its' own feel and even its taste to it, and I never really appreciated it until now.

A few cats said what's up to me when I stepped out of the station. They were young cats, teenagers. The girls openly stared at me like I was dinner, while a couple of cats eyed me suspiciously. No doubt they were hustlers.

I felt too good to show them they weren't as tough as they thought. I kept the smile on my face, said what's up to the cats that greeted me, and winked at a couple of the young tenda while I headed to my destination. I didn't mind the walk, and it allowed me to take in all that had changed.

I walked to the San Pablo Bart Station and rode the Bart to East Oakland, and I got off at the Coliseum stop. The ride only took a few minutes, but I got a somewhat ariel view of the change the city had undergone in my absence. I was utterly shocked.

Shock turned into bereavement as I walked down the street after exiting the Coliseum Station. I couldn't believe the level of deterioration that had fallen over my once beautiful city in such a short time. I hadn't even been gone four years, yet it felt like I was looking at Oakland for the first time in over ten grueling years. By the time I reached the street of my destination, my heart was bursting with sorrow and sympathy for the death of the greatest city I had ever known. I was even more determined to succeed in the cause that The Brotha's believed in. I was ready to right some wrongs.

The house I was reporting to check in, was an old house but I could tell that it was well taken care of. The blue and white paint on the outside of the house could have been no more than a couple of years old. Judging by the sturdiness of the chain link fence that was in front of the house. I would guess the gate was fairly new as well. Most likely installed around the same time that the house was painted.

There were a few Brotha's hanging out in front of the house. To an outsider, it would appear they were just that young brotha hanging out. However, I had been trained to see what other people didn't see. Like the way all their eyes methodically scanned the block. Reading and analyzing everything. I noticed how all of them kept one of their hands either in a jacket pocket or waistband. Most likely close to their guns that were hidden from the plain eye. Lastly, I noticed they all stood and moved in a way that would suggest that they were in good physical shape. This was due to the mandatory daily exercise regimen and structure. These were indeed young soldiers who were a part of the Usalama or security squad.

As I moved towards the gate, all their attention had diverted to me. Tension aroused as they eyed me differently. A few brief words were exchanged and instantly all tension disappeared. I was asked a few questions, all of which I was prepared for, and gave the correct responses.

One of them lead me into the house and told me to have a seat, while he disappeared down a hallway. The Brotha's owned several houses throughout the city being used for bases or operating offices. One of them served as headquarters for the Oakland Chapter.

After a few minutes, the kid that let me into the house came walking from out the back. He didn't speak to me nor stop; he walked right out of the front door; I assumed to go back to his post.

I just sat there and waited a little while longer until I heard his footsteps coming down the hall and that's when I saw him. The footsteps sounded like they belonged to a giant. Like when Bugs Bunny had climbed the beanstalk and entered the giant castle in the cartoon. I swear even the couch that I was sitting on was vibrating.

When he finally emerged from the hallway, I stood up instinctively. I was face to face with the biggest man I had ever seen. He had to stand at least seven feet tall and looked to weigh 340 to 380 pounds of solid muscle. This mothafucka was beyond huge. He in fact could very well be the giant from Jack in The Beanstalk. Even at 6'4" I had to crane my neck backward to look into his face. I wasn't the cowering type, so I stood my ground and looked him in his eyes.

"Big Joe, I gotta tell you that I wasn't expecting you for another day or so. Most guys take advantage of the full 72 hours they have to check in." He stepped to me and extended his hand for a shake. "Names Vick, but everybody calls me Tiny Africa." His voice resembled thunder or the sound a volcano makes when it erupts.

I didn't see any reason to say my name when he had already used it. So instead, I told him, "I don't like to procrastinate. I prefer dealing with things as soon as they arise, or as soon as time allows." His hand was the size of a catcher's mitt and had a nice firm grip. "I heard a lot of good things about you from The Brotha's. They say your Cadre is involved in some heavy moves that are the kind of moves that both the party and the people need. If that's really how it's going down, then I want to be a part of it."

He looked at me hard for a long while as if he was reading and studying me. Analyzing and dissecting what I'd just told him. Probably wondering not only if I was sincere but also weighing in his mind if I was ready for what I was asking for or not.

He chuckled. "So, you ready for some real work? Ready to get your feet wet?" He asked me.

I didn't know if he asked everyone this same question the way he was asking me, but for some reason, it felt like he was personally challenging me. Daring me to say I was ready.

"That's exactly what I signed up for, straight and to the point". I wasn't going to beat around the bush or sing and dance for him.

"Joe this isn't that peaceful protest, The Brotha's that God forgave type shit. My Cadre is heavily involved in that Cambon Black Guerilla Family shit! We take the fight straight to the enemy regardless of who the enemy is. Race, color, creed, that shit don't mean nothing to us. We will actively combat and neutralize any threat to the party or the party's ability to carry forth its' works, objectives, or policies. Our hands get dirty!" He stared at me with that look again like he was studying me.

Again, he chuckled. Even his laugh sounded like it was testing me. Calling me out and goading me into taking the bait that he was dangling in front of me.

"Blood I've been getting my hands dirty from the moment I learned how to use them. I'mma stand up brotha. Straight forward. I shoot from the hip. I let my yeses be yes and my no's be no's. And when I commit to something then I'm all in no hesitation, no questions asked." This time I matched his hard stare with one of my own.

A fire lit in his eyes. I could tell he was impressed, the read on his analysis came back and he liked what he received.

"Alright Big Joe, come on follow me." He turned around without waiting to see if I would reply. He walked away without wondering if I would follow or not.

I followed him through the door and down some stairs into a basement. I could hear the soft murmur of voices as we descended the steps. Of course, I couldn't see past the gigantic frame of Tiny Africa. Once we reached the bottom of the stairs, Tiny Africa continued to proceed into the basement.

There was complete lighting in the basement, and I could see the entire room good. Two long couches were along the east and west walls, and with recliners, at their edges, the furniture formed a rectangular shape. On the wall directly facing me was a banner. The banner was the same color, green as the pool table's cloth. A giant fierce-looking black dragon was in the center of the banner. Above the dragon in big red block letters were the words, The Black Guerilla with Family under the dragon. All throughout the basement were African decorations. Ranging from East African shields and spears, tribal masks, and animal prints to weird sculptures that I couldn't make out.

There were about eight or nine serious-looking brotha's seated on the furniture. One brotha was over by a portable refrigerator next to a table in the corner. All of them had stopped whatever it was they were doing before us coming down the stairs. Now they were all openly staring at me. Some with hostility, some with indifference; I could tell all of them were reading me, wondering what my place was and why I was invited into their personal domain. I gave each man enough stare back to let them know that wasn't no bitch over here. But not enough to challenge anyone.

"Say everybody, this here is our Brotha Big Joe. He just did three years behind the walls at Quentin with Joker Askari (Ah-scar-ee) and A.C. They've spoken nothing but good about the brotha. He just got out a few hours ago, and instead of tasting freedom first, like most people do, he came straight here. To me, any brotha showing that level of commitment and dedication deserves a chance to function with and become a part of a Cadre that's really pushing our organizational ideologies and policies to the fullest. I want y'all to embrace the brotha like we all embrace each other." When Tiny Africa addressed the room, he spoke in a way that commanded attention, and his tone and voice commanded obedience.

One by one all of the brotha's introduced themselves to me, the looks of hostility were gone. A couple of the brotha's told me that I would receive a certain level of respect based on the fact that I was part of Joker Askari's and A.C.'s Cadre. Those two names carried a lot of weight and respect in the organization.

I spent the better part of half of the day down in that basement getting to know the brotha's. Sharing ideological views, political policies, and ways to help and better the people. Little did I know they were all testing, reading, and judging me to see if I was ready for their level of Revolutionary Tactics. Little did they know, the fire that burned in me was hotter than the center vortex of Hell. They weren't ready for my level of Revolution period.

CHAPTER 4

I left the clubhouse in the east and rode the Bart back over to West Oakland. One of the Brotha's offered to give me a ride, but I declined. Being a part of a group or an organization was a new experience for me. I was used to being a lone wolf, and that's how I've spent most of my life. Therefore, since taking my oath in prison and becoming a part of a collective, I've come to welcome the moments of solidarity that I received. Plus, until I come to fully trust the Cadre that was sent to me, I was going to exercise extreme caution with them as well. They didn't need to know too much about me until I'd learned more about them.

It was already dark by the time I made it home. Needless to say, my old lady Carla was pissed. When I didn't show up at a reasonable time, she let her mind run wild with all sorts of infidelity. I could never cheat on her though. She's the only woman my eyes have ever noticed since high school. I reminded her of this as well as how deeply in love with her that I am.

Once I calmed her down, we talked and then made love all night, stopping only to eat and drink. The years that we were denied the chance to make love to one another were hard as hell. We did our best to try and make up for the lost time in a single night as we finally collapsed due to exhaustion.

I didn't wake up the following day until well after noon, but Carla was already up. She had cleaned the house and was putting the finishing touches on breakfast. I think it was the smell of food that awakened me. It felt good to wake up in a nice soft, warm bed instead of a cold hard prison bunk inside of a concrete cell.

Carla didn't join me in eating, she said she would eat later. She was just enjoying watching me scoff down her meal like it was the best food on earth. At that moment, to me it was. We talked for a little bit while I ate breakfast. She made waffles with a homemade Blueberry sauce with real Blueberries. Thick juicy slices of bacon, scrambled eggs with cheese, and homemade potatoes. This was better than any food from any restaurant.

After my belly was full, I asked her about her mom, she said she had been staying with her mom for a while. She didn't elaborate, so I left it at that for now but thought to myself I need to revisit that.

I told Carla that I wanted to stop by The Brotha's. I was dead serious about becoming a part of the solution to the plight that had befallen our people. I had contributed to that plight before going to prison by selling that poison to our people. Now I planned to do any and everything I could to rectify the wrong that I had done. Carla told me that she was proud of me beyond belief. She even told me to take her car so I wouldn't have to depend on public transportation.

She had an old-school grey 1972 Cutlass that was rundown, but it started up when I turned the key, and I could feel its power underneath me as I drove. I couldn't believe how bad the city had turned. I mean it had gone to shit. The once beautiful family neighborhood had become something out of one of the Hollywood zombie movies. The ones where cities are ruined and abandoned. It was hard to fathom that something as small as a piece of crack rock being able to alter a town and so many lives in such a drastic way. But that is what happened.

I was let into the house by one of the brotha's that was down in the basement last night. I remembered his name was Weusi (Way-oo-see) Askari, which meant the Black Warrior. I would later find out he was Tiny Africa's Minister of Security, which meant he was in charge of guns and weapons, personnel detail, and any and everything that had to do with the security of the Cadre. Including the young cats that were outside keeping a lookout.

Weusi Askari led the way thru the house and down into the basement. Tiny Africa was in the middle of some kind of speech when we came down the stairs. He was standing off by the back table and refrigerator, so he was facing the whole room. I took a few steps to the right once I was off the stairs and listened. His deep baritone voice demanded my attention. His words were intoxicating.

".... My Brotha's don't think for one second that change or Revolution will come thru peace and love. Singing old hymns of Kumbaya and we shall overcome. Nothing worth achieving was ever reached thru dreams and wishes. You can dream all you want but unless you put some action behind those dreams, you'll be waiting on a fairy tale ending forever. To change something, you must change it! In order Forhieve Revolution, we must fight to achieve it! The white man doesn't give a fuck about our plight in the inner-city ghettos. We are slowly helping them achieve their goal, the eradication, and annihilation of the black man's mind. They feed these drugs in our communities with hopes of them doing exactly what they are doing. Destroying our minds. Our own personal inadeelf-hatred have taken their plans to another level. We are destroying ourselves! And doing so at a rate faster than white man ever could have done." He paused to allow each man inside the basement to weigh what he just said. "The threat now comes from within. That's why it's up to us not up to any outsiders, but up to us to restore the balance to bring some balance back to the ghetto. And for us to do this, we first must get rid of the problem. There's no way for us to expect the people to ever get over their sickness if the stuff that is poisoning them is still right there in the hood. My brotha's it is up to us. It's our jobs as Vanguards of the people to be not only the voice of the people but also the right arm of vindication. We are the urban guerilla, and we must fight for our people! The Revolution is here and we as guerillas are its fighters." When he finished speaking everyone began clapping.

I hadn't known how long he'd spoke, but what I had heard was powerful enough to give that flame that was burning within me some added fuel. I was ready to do something. Anything, as long as it was in the name of the Party and what we were fighting for. I mentioned this to Tiny Africa. He looked at me in that strange way of reading me that he had, a smile slowly spread across his face, and he told me that we would discuss it after everyone left.

A couple of hours later everyone had left, it was only Tiny Africa and me down in the basement. He'd waited until the last person left to go over to the refrigerator and grab a couple of cans of Old English. He walked over to the couch I was seated on and handed me a can, then he sat down next to me on the couch. After all the talking I had just done to all the different comrades, a nice cold beer was exactly what I needed.

"Big Joe, so you think you're ready to do your part and start helping to clean up the city?" He asked me. His voice was soft, yet his stare was intense.

"Tiny, I've already been doing my part. Even from the inside, I did my part. I'm ready to do more. I need to be doing more." I was beyond being committed. I was yearning to right the wrongs I was a part of. I was desperate.

Instantly he asked. "How far would go to help your people? To protect your people, Big Joe how far would you go to save your people?"

I didn't have to think about it. Not at all! Not for one second. "As far as it is needed for me to go."

"Would you rob or steal? Kill if you had to?" The question probably would have thrown some niggas off. But I'm from the killing fields of West Oakland so that shit didn't faze me.

"I've already done all of that and some while I was foolishly hurting my people. I'm willing to do more than that if it will help my people.

He leaned back and looked straight ahead. I could tell he was thinking about what I told him. He just sat there, quiet for a long time, and I didn't feel the need to say anything else, so I just waited. We must have sat there for a good four or five minutes before finally, he got up. Still, he didn't say a word to me, he climbed the stairs out of the basement.

For a minute I wondered if I had made a mistake or if I may have said something that I shouldn't have said. He came back downstairs almost immediately. He was holding a block pager in his left hand. He gave me the pager and told me to never turn it off and to always make sure that the battery was charged. I could use the pager as my own personal pager. But if I ever received the code 276, I was to stop whatever I was doing and get over to The Club House which was the official name of the house we were at.

None of that would be a problem for me and I let Africa know that. We sat and talked for about another hour or so about Revolution and the things that must be done in order to achieve Revolution. We both understood that without sacrifice there could be no gain. Everyone was constantly screaming that we needed change, yet no one was willing to stand up and create change. Tiny Africa and his Cadre were changing that. They were doing more than just standing up, they were making changes, and I wanted to be a part of that change. I left The Club House that night feeling that the decision I made telling Tiny Africa that I wanted to do more would alter my life drastically.

Finding out just how much my life was going to be affected and altered didn't take long at all. Not even a week had gone by before I got the page with the code 276. I was at the house listening to the new E-40 and The Click album while I was cutting the grass. The lawn mower was an old gas diesel mower that kept cutting off on me because the grass was so long. Every time it cut off on me, I would pause my Walkman before adjusting the levers on the mower. It was during one of these times that I heard the pager going off. The page couldn't have come at a better time, it was getting hot as hell, and I was tired. I put the lawn mower up, told Carla I had to take care of something, jumped in her car, and took off.

It didn't take me long to pull up in front of the house. I no longer needed an escort inside. The young brotha's out front acknowledged me with a head nod and went on about their business. As I expected, everyone was in the basement. Six brotha's sat on the couches. Four of whom I'd met before, two were new to me. The energy inside the room let me know these were some serious brotha's. It also told me that this meeting was not casual. There were no jokes or smiles in the room.

"Well, my brotha, you asked for the next step in the fight for revolution; said you was ready. Well, tonight you're gonna get your chance." Tiny Afrika spoke in a low voice. He came and stood off to my side.

"What's going on tonight?" I asked. A part of me knew the answer already. Still, I wanted to hear him say it.

"Tonight, we're going to clean up the streets. We're gonna rid the town of some Philistines!"

The look in his eyes was cold as steel. A chill traveled down my spine.

A Philistine was worse than an Uncle Tom. He was an agent of provocateur, a threat to himself and the people but doesn't know it. He is someone who misbelieves that he is in control of his destiny. Not realizing that control of his life has been out of his hands for a long time. Drug dealers, confidential and paid informants, snitches, and blood-sucking pimps are a couple of examples of Philistines. They were poison and all deserved their fate.

I just nodded my head in agreement. There was no need to say anything. Shit, what was I going to say anyway? I'd signed up for this. I needed to correct my wrongs. Needed to make up for what I did to Carla.

"Listen up!" Tiny Africa said, getting everyone's attention. "Like I always say, less is best. So, we don't need a whole lot of talking. We all know what the bizzness is and we all know what we got to do. So, let's get it done. For you, Brotha's that haven't been here this past week, this Brotha here is Big Joe. Big Joe is fresh out of the bricks and is eager to build the party. He rolling out with us tonight. Bout to get his feet wet!

When he was done talking, Tiny Africa made his way back over to me with a Brotha named Simba. After introducing us, he explained to me that Simba would be the driver of one of the cars. I would be the passenger in that car. I had the most important job he told me. I was their eyes and ears. Didn't matter to me because I knew I would have to prove myself here just like anywhere else.

Simba gave me the low down on what exactly was popping off. We were hitting a drug house. Everybody was to die. No survivors were the rules. My job would be a simple one. While they bum-rushed the spot, I was supposed to keep Usalama outside. I was to make sure nobody got in or out of the spot once they went in. They would be blind when they were ready to come out of the house. Which is why they needed me to make sure they didn't run into any problems.

We rode in two separate cars. I was shotgun in the lead car like Tiny Africa said. A brotha by the name of Bebe (Bay-Bay) road along with me and Simba. We listened to Tupac Shakur's new album *Strictly 4 My N.I.G.G.A.Z.* The volume was low as we drove through the city. Each man was lost in his own thoughts.

When we made it to the house, Simba pulled over and parked two houses down. As planned, I wanted a full minute after Bebe had gotten out of the car before I stepped out. The first thing I did was scan the block looking for any sign of movement at all. I made my way to the edge of the property line and posted up. I didn't want to be directly in front of the house in case any stray bullets came flying thru the walls. Shit sounded like World War III was popping off right in the middle of East Oakland.

The sounds weren't new to us. Being from Oakland we all were used to gunshots every night. The street was empty, which was a good thing. The first thing you learned coming up in Oakland California was to mind your business. Whenever gunshots erupt in the night, niggaz knew to get the fuck outta dodge. That's what sensible people do. So, if

I would have seen anybody on the street, it would've been a problem, because they would've been a problem.

I looked towards Simba in the car down the street. I could make out his silhouette in the driver's seat. His head was on a swivel as he kept his own Usalama. A noise to my left alerted my attention back to the house. The front door was open, and somebody was coming through the door. It was one of the rads. As I was looking at him, movement out the corner of my eye caught my attention. This alerted me because there should not have been any movement over there. The area I was looking at was the side of the house.

The bushes that ran down the length of the side of the house, made it even darker. My night vision was on point, that's how I was able to spot him. A nigga was crouched down hiding in the shadows. The movement I saw was him standing up and peeking around the side of the house. No doubt he was trying to get the drop on the brotha's that were coming out of the front door.

Either he hadn't seen me, or he didn't give two fucks about me. Either way, ignoring me would prove fatal. My Glock 17 had already been cocked and loaded. Without hesitation, I aimed at the dark figure and started firing. I barely caught a glance of the comrade that was coming out of the house as he ducked low and raised his gun. No doubt my first thought, I was a possible threat.

It didn't matter I was already moving. I was running towards the body of the nigga I was shooting. From the way the body fell, I knew I'd hit him. I was still running because I didn't know if there were more shooters back there or what. The nigga laying on the ground was the only one hiding on the side of the house.

Tiny Africa was the last person out of the house. We made eye contact as I stepped over the body. He looked down at the body and back into my eyes. He nodded his head in approval before jogging off. I jogged back to Simba, who didn't waste any time pulling off. Both cars drove in opposite directions back to the Club House...

The atmosphere inside was calm and mellow. If I had not personally been there with them, there's no way I would've believed that these guys had just come from killing however many people we killed back there. Somebody handed me a glass of alcohol, which I gratefully accepted. While I was savoring the feel of the alcohol's smooth burn as it made its way down my throat, Tiny Africa called over to me and said, "Good job out there." Those words were the only acknowledgments or comments about what we'd done that night.

CHAPTER 5

I made it back to Carla's at almost two in the morning to find all of the lights on and Bobby Brown singing about needing his girlfriend. When I walked to the back room her back was to me. She held a crack pipe in one hand and a lighter in the other. She was slowly shaking her head while she swayed her hips to the rhythm of the song wearing nothing but her bra and panties.

I had no control, tears welled up in my eyes. I could easily smell the pungent sweet odor of the crack. The smell was thick and heavy. I didn't know what to do. My baby was a crackhead. How in the fuck was a nigga supposed to take this shit? How in the fuck did this happen? When? All sorts of thoughts raced through a niggaz mind so fast, I couldn't hold onto them.

The tears escaped my eyes as she put the glass pipe to her lips and took a hit. I was paralyzed with anger. I wanted to kill a mothafucka! Anybody! But there wasn't anyone around but my Baby. Ray Charles could see that right now she needed me. I walked up to her and wrapped my arms around her.

"Sssh Carla, it's me, baby." I kissed her softly on her neck calming her down some. Her neck was moist from sweat. I didn't even think of the possibility of scaring her or her paranoia from the drugs.

"Ooh hey Daddy. Mm, I see you came home ready for some of this good pussy tonight." She grinded her ass into me slowly and sensually.

Her movements weren't the same. She moved like a completely different person.

"Baby you can't be putting that poison in your body." She swayed her hips to the beat and hummed along with the song like she didn't hear anything I said.

"Mm mm.... baby poison doesn't make you feel this good.... Girlfriend, and I need you right now. Come on Daddy sing with me." She was trying to turn around in my arms.

I was too scared of what she would look like in this condition, so I just held her as tight as I could as the tears rolled down my cheeks. "Mm mm.... That's right Daddy." She moaned. "I know what you want. Hold Mama tight baby." As I held her in my arms, she put the lighter in the other hand with the pipe. Then she put her free hand down inside the front of her panties.

Just like that, while listening to Bobby sing, in my arms she began playing with herself. Her swaying and grinding slowed down. She was moving to her own rhythm. I got angry at myself for getting excited but fuck I couldn't help it. This was my old lady and the way her soft ass felt as it grinded up against me had me rock hard. But I couldn't play myself like that. I kissed and gently bit down on her sweaty neck softly.

"Baby come to take a shower with me." I did my best Luther Vandross impersonation as I whispered into her ear.

"Mm mm.... first kiss me, Daddy." She spoke seductively.

This time I allowed her to turn around in my arms. I brought my lips to hers and gave her a soft kiss. It was horrible. I could taste the chemical taste of the crack residue on her lips along with the stale taste of tobacco. My Baby didn't even smoke cigarettes. At least I thought she didn't. The experience brought more pain to my heart. I let the pain out through my kiss as more tears flowed down my cheeks. I kissed Carla with more passion releasing some of my pain. I needed her to know that I was there with her no matter what. Just as she had stood by my side and in my corner during my bid, I would be there for her standing tall in her corner throughout her battle with this sickness.

How could I look down on or judge this woman? This woman who had gone through so much shit and put up with even more just to stay loyal to me and by my side. The kiss became symbolic to me. It was filled with our needs. Her need for my love and support and my need for her to understand that I didn't know what made her weak enough to run to drugs. But I understood her pain, and I needed her just as badly as she needed me.

We didn't make it to the bathroom. I kissed her all over her salty, sweaty body while we made love.

Afterward, we just lay there for hours talking. I'm not the type of person to ignore shit or sweep it under the rug. I steered the conversation towards her using drugs. I wanted to know everything. How she started. Why did she start? Did somebody force her the first time? All the questions a man whose woman was on drugs could think to ask. I was beyond ready to kill any mothafucka if she gave me a name. If someone was responsible for my wife sucking on a glass dick, he would be dead by the end of the week.

What I wasn't ready for was the truth that she told me. It was me. I was the cause of my own pain. I was the one responsible for the weakness that sent her to the crack pipe. She told me that she was miserable and lonely with me behind bars and that she didn't know what to do. She put up with the disrespect and humiliation that the prison guards made her go through every time she would come to visit because she was my woman and that's what she was supposed to do. But she never told me because she knew what I would do and she didn't want me to get into trouble, which I did anyway. I was constantly getting into trouble behind The Cause or The Family. She understood all about being a revolutionary and fighting for the cause. But that didn't help numb the pain she felt behind not knowing when I would finally make it home. If I would make it home.

Carla told me that the last time I was sent to the hole in prison for stabbing a Comrade that turned against The Family, she broke down for three whole days straight. I was facing attempted murder charges and she believed I was going to get life in prison. On the third day in a hazy depressing cloud of sorrow, she made her way on foot to the nearest D-Boy she could find. She came home and drowned her pain and sorrow in the cloud of crack smoke and Cisco wine coolers.

By the time she was done telling me everything, we both were silently shedding tears. I just held her in my arms until the exhaustion of our lovemaking and pouring her heart out took its effects and she fell asleep.

CHAPTER 6
(Present Day: Ty Dollar-Sign)

I sat at the dining room table across from my Pops waiting for him to continue the story. Instead, he just sat there with a sad, blank expression on his face. I didn't know how I was supposed to take the information he shared with me.

For a long time, I often wondered what could drive a strong black woman an active participant in The Black Panther Party to the sharp fierce clutches of crack. When I was younger, I desperately needed to know what was strong enough to weaken someone so much that they could easily abandon their child like mom abandoned me.... Now I know.

"Say, old man, you alright?" I usually called him old man instead of Pops whenever I was feeling some kind of way.

He blinked a couple of times coming out of his daze. He stared at me for a moment before saying, "I-I need some rest son. I-I'm alright. I just need to lay down and rest for a minute. Come back tomorrow and I'll pick up where I left off."

I was hesitant to leave him alone under the circumstances but considering my confusion I figured it was best. I let him know that if needed me for anything, all he had to do was call me. Then I dipped.

Later I found myself sitting on my couch with a fifth of Remy in my hands. Too many thoughts were going through my mind for me to sleep. Old memories of my mom that a nigga had buried resurfaced. I wasn't ashamed of the tears that fell down my face. I just didn't understand them.

My mom's wasn't a part of my life. She had been smoked out for as long as I could remember. My grandmother had been the only mother that I knew. She was the woman that raised me. The one I called mom. Yet for some reason after hearing how Carla got started smoking dope, I couldn't help feeling sorry for her. She must've loved Pops if being away from him was that hard on her. I couldn't imagine anybody having that much power or influence over me.

I titled the bottle and guzzled almost a third of the Remy trying my best to erase the pain that didn't belong to me.

I remember when I was younger my aunty Elaine used to tell me all kinds of positive stories about my mom's. Stories from their Black Panther days. Elaine used to say that moms had been one of the strongest sistah in the movement. She told me my mom would organize some of the biggest and most influential rallies' that they had.

Equality and Social Justice for all people were just a couple of things that The Party stood for. Moms was the first one to come up with the idea of feeding the community. Along with organizing coat and jacket drives for the kids in the community that needed them.

The stories that aunty Elaine use to tell me about moms were a complete contradiction from the things I remembered as a kid when you're going thru the shit that I went thru. Growing up with a dad in prison and a dope fiend for a mom you barely remember moments of enjoyment because they rarely occurred. If they occurred at all.

For a moment, I thought about calling Laurice sexy ass to come over and help take my mind off the madness that was going on inside my head. Instead, I rolled a blunt of that Grand-Daddy and turned on the television.

The sound of my cell phone woke me up. I don't remember dozing off. Instead of picking up my phone, I searched for the Backwoods I had been smoking on. Somehow, I was sitting on it. I guess it's a good thing I didn't drop it and fuck around and burn this bitch down while I was sleeping.

I jumped in the shower and got dressed. After I left the house, I stopped and picked up some breakfast before I made my way over to Pop's house. I called twice but he didn't answer. It didn't matter though. I was on my way over to his spot regardless. He told me that he needed to get this shit off his chest, and I was going to let him do just that.

He answered the door wearing the same shit he was wearing when I left. I didn't say shit about it. Pops had the heater on but somehow the house felt cold. Not a chilly cold but that cold you feel when you're all alone in an empty place. I could smell the strong odor of cleaning supplies in the air. I wondered if he had decided to clean the house instead of going to sleep last night. Again, I kept my thoughts to myself as I followed him in.

I separated the food once we got to the dining room. I looked over in the kitchen. I didn't see the dishes that I'd seen last night and the table in the dining room looked freshly wiped down, confirming my thoughts about him cleaning.

"How you feeling this morning Pops?" I asked him as I sat down.

He didn't answer me. Instead, he picked up the tall cup of coffee I put in front of him and took a big swallow. Which fucked me up because the shit was still piping hot. He picked up his fork and started eating his food quietly. I figured he would talk whenever he was ready. So, I started eating my food too. When I was younger getting to eat breakfast was rarer than finding a four-leaf clover. I guess that's the reason it's my favorite meal now.

"Now I don't want you coming around here, talking to me and asking all these sentimental ass questions just cause you know I'm dying." He interrupted my thoughts with his deep voice. "Aint no reason to be feeling sorry for me. Shit death ain't no worse than life. It might be better since you ain't got to deal with a whole lot of bullshit no more." He ate a piece of bacon and then added. "So, don't come up in here asking me how I'm doing. Shit, I'm doing!"

I shoveled a fork full of scrambled eggs into my mouth. I looked at him like he'd lost his muthafucka's mind while I chewed. After a few seconds, I responded. "Yeah, a 'right I got you on that. But while we're setting the record straight, why don't you keep in mind that you ain't talking to no little kid either." Dying or not, a mothafucka was going to respect me. Straight up!

"Well, now that the bullshit is all out of the way, maybe we can eat this good food without any problems." Pops stuffed his mouth with some of the blueberry banana pancakes.

The only reason I didn't say nothing was because my phone went off. When I pulled it out to check and see who was getting at me, I noticed I had a text message from my nigga Keak. He wanted to know if I wanted to roll with him to the Bay Area Rap Scene Awards. The BARS Awards were known to be popping. I shot a message back letting him know it was all good. Then I got busy with my food before it got cold.

About ten minutes later, Pops just started telling his story again like it never stopped.

"Tiny Africa had gotten word that there was a heroin distribution center in West Oakland. Crack was the number one dope being sold and used, yet there was still plenty of people strung out on the hop too.

The word we got was there were only a few women inside of the house cutting and bagging the dope. There wouldn't be no more than eight women in the house along with one armed guard. He was responsible for making sure the women didn't try and steal any dope as well as keeping the place safe.

We decided that since there was only supposed to be one dude and a bunch of chicks, only Tiny Africa, me and Simba, and I needed to go. We'd go in there, disarm the guard and destroy all of the dope. It would be one more victory for us in the battle to clean up the community.

The house turned out to be a single-story 3-bedroom with two big windows in the front of the house and none in the back. We got into the house as easily as if we owned the place ourselves. There were six girls in the house seated around a long folding table that was in the dining room area.

The women were all in their panties without bras seated at the table packaging the dope in little, small $5 and $10 bundles. None of them made a peep when we came in. They were so high, that they only paused long enough to look at us when we came in. Then they went right back to doing what they were doing like we weren't there.

I searched the entire house for the guard but didn't find him anywhere. There was one room I couldn't check it had a padlock on the door. I made it back to the front of the house and I told Tiny Africa that I hadn't located the guy that was supposed to be on guard.

He stepped to the closest sistah to him. She was a deep dark chocolate sistah with a nice afro. Her titties were huge. They sat perfectly on her chest with nice, mouth-watering gum drop nipples. He asked her where was the guy that was supposed to be there. She wiped some perspiration off of her face with the back of her hand and ended up getting some of the powdered heroin on her face. She told Tiny Africa that the guy had one of the girls down in the basement. Each night he would choose a different girl to take down there and have sex with them. Even though they didn't like it, they were making way too much money to tell him no. Simba went to get them.

I used the time he was gone to really get a look at everything. One sistah was cutting pure heroin with lactose and powdered milk. She was a plump light-skinned cutie pie with a fat ass. There was what looked to be at least three or four kilos already blended spread along the table ready and waiting to be packaged. Though all of the sistahs looked high, none of them looked like junkies. Since none of them were wearing masks, I figured they were getting high from breathing it in. I actually took a step backward away from the table.

Simba came back with the guard and a skinny light skinned sistah that looked like she was seventeen. They were both completely naked and sweaty. By then the women were no longer working. They just sat there looking confused and slightly amused that the guard had got slipping.

"I'ma go check that room that got the lock on it now that we got everything under control." I didn't address anyone in particular; I just spoke out loud.

When I got to the door, I used the butt of the shotgun I was holding to break the lock off. I slowly pushed the door open. I had to find the light switch and turn it on to see. The room was empty except for a few boxes that were on the floor. I figured they contained more drugs. When I opened one of the boxes, I froze. The last thing I expected to be in the box is what was actually in it. I checked all the other boxes and found the same shit.

I picked one of the boxes up and walked back out into the front room. The women were getting dressed.

"What's in the box?" Tiny Africa asked when he saw me carrying the box.

"Have a look." I set the box down in one of the empty chairs.

"God Damn!" That was all Tiny Africa could say after looking into the cardboard box full of cash.

"This was in that room and there's several more boxes back there," I told him.

"H-How many more?"

There were seven boxes all together all filled with cash. Tiny Africa kept an eye on the dude who was supposed to be on guard and the sistahs, while me and Simba loaded the boxes into the ride, we were in. Before we took the last box out, we stuffed as much cash into the sistah's purses as we could. That way they would be straight until they found another gig. Then we poured gasoline all over the inside of the house and torched it. We made the guard run down the street asshole butt naked while we drove off in the opposite direction.

When word about the lick got out, it spread through the streets of Oakland like wildfire. All sorts of rumors were being thrown out there. I even heard that everyone in the house was burned alive. Supposedly there was two and a half mill inside the spot. It was crazy.

In truth, we came away with over a half mill. We went back and forth over what we should do with the money for a long time. We ended up giving ten grand to each of the brothas in the Cadre. It was like showing them we appreciated the personal sacrifices that they made to support the party and fight for The Cause. We put the rest of the money into the people like we were supposed to do.

I reached out to Carla's older sister Elaine, her and Carla were both members of The Panthers. In fact, at one time Elaine was the Chairman of the entire party. I asked her if she wouldn't mind helping us organize a clothes and food drive. Elaine was always for the people. She'd been that way ever since I'd known her. She didn't hesitate to help us.

Around this time E-40 had taken the Blueprint on the independent rap game to a whole other level. A few Cats before E-40 had done the independent thang, but no one had taken it to the level that he did. Too Short was another major player. He opened up doors for up-and-coming rappers. He was the biggest rapper in Oakland. There were a bunch of young cats all wanting to be like Too Short and his crew. We decided to help a few brothas join the rap game. This way not only could we help a brotha make it, but in return, they would give back. Supporting our motto of *"Each One Meet One, Each One Greet One, Each One Teach One."*

We had a comrade up under another Cadre that followed the Islamic laws and teachings. His name was Ansar Muhammad. He had a young comrade under his Cadre who was exceptional with his understanding of revolutionary doctrine and had a very unique and direct way of expressing that through his music. The young brotha's name was Askari X. He already had two tapes out. *Word of the State* and *Message to the Black Man*. While I was in prison, I had heard his *Word of The State* album, it was powerful.

I reached out to Ansar to try and see about possibly working on a project together. When I finally linked up with the brotha he provided me with some very disturbing and heartbreaking news. Apparently, someone either jealous of the brotha's influence or intimidated by his message slipped Askari X a Mickey. The young brotha's mind wasn't quite the same after that.

Word was starting to spread internally about an investigation being done on the comrade Seagram. The investigation was in regard to an allegation made by another comrade that supposedly Seagram had made a statement in an open case. It didn't matter if the allegations were true or not. The investigation would settle that. All that mattered for us was we couldn't risk the negative energy from the situation running over to us and what we were trying to do.

With all this going on things weren't any better at home. Carla had become a full crackhead. The occasional usage she had been doing when I came home gave way to her smoking every chance she got. I came home one night to find her seated in the dark on the couch crying like a child. When I turned the lights on tears welled up in my eyes and anger took over my body.

Her clothes were dirty and raggedy. They looked like she had been wearing them for weeks. Her hair was all over the place. My attention was drawn to her face. It looked like a mothafucka beat my baby with a sock full of quarters. One eye was swollen completely shut. The other was blood red. Signs that a blood vessel had been ruptured in it. Her nose had caked up dried blood in her nostrils and her lips were busted.

I quickly rushed over to her and fell to my knees. The sight of her in pain brought tears to my eyes. She was in dire need of a shower, but I ignored the strong musky smell. Over and over, I asked her who had done this to her. As I cried, I swore to my baby that I would make whoever had touched her pay dearly for what they had done. Her crying intensified and the sounds of her sobs shattered my heart.

Since I wasn't getting anywhere questioning her. I got up off my knees, sat down next to her, and held her in my arms. I continued to tell her it would be okay while I held her and gently rocked her back and forth. All kinds of murderous thoughts kept going through my mind. What she had done to deserve this never entered my mind. Because a real man knows that there's nothing a woman could ever do to be beaten like she was a man. Nothing! I was so furious that my body was trembling. I forced myself to concentrate on controlling the trembling. After all, this wasn't about me or my rage. It was about Carla and what had been done to her.

I don't know how long we sat there on the couch before Carla opened up and told me what had happened to her and why. My rage not only returned but it had multiplied. She told me that she had owed some cat for some dope. It wasn't the first time that she had owed him. Apparently, she had been buying dope from him enough that he often fronted the dope to her. According to Carla, one time when she couldn't pay the debt that she owed, the nigga raped her.

He was the only D-Boy that would give her dope on credit, so she went back to him. This time when she couldn't pay him the $40 that she owed him, she'd offered to suck his dick. I didn't know how to take hearing some shit like that from the woman I loved. It made me wonder about all the shit she could've been out on the streets doing. She was the love of my life though. Plus, she had stood tall by my side. She stayed in my corner throughout my prison bid. I pushed that shit out of my mind and focused on her.

When she offered to suck his dick, the nigga laughed at her and told her that she had disrespected him. Then he beat the shit out of her right there in front of everybody. Carla cried even harder as she told me how everybody laughed at her while the nigga beat her. She told me the name of the nigga, and I knew exactly who he was.

This was about to be a huge problem. One that I didn't cause, but one that I would solve. He was from East Oakland but was known to hangout in the West. He was also family. I'm not talking cousin, uncle, or brother. He wasn't a relative. He was a member of The Black Guerilla Family as I was. He was family.

CHAPTER 7

Had this been a normal nigga; I would've handled my business and that would've been it. This was a supposed comrade. Therefore, after spending that night and the following day and night tending to Carla. Making sure she was okay. I went to go see Tiny Africa and told him everything. I knew he would be pissed to hear about a comrade pushing that poison to our people.

I was shocked to learn that Tiny Africa had already known about the cat. He was part of a Cadre that was under this new regime that felt it was okay to sell dope as a means to generate income that would help The Family attain its goals and agenda. He told me that there had been tension between the old regime and the new regime behind this for quite some time. I had heard about the tension back in prison. I never knew that it was behind dope.

Tiny Africa set up a meeting with the "C" of that Cadre. The "C" was what we called the overseer. The head nigga in charge. After the meeting was set, we called up eight comrades from our Cadre and had them all come to The Club House. When they got there, we ran down to them what was up. By this time, I had been a functioning member of their Cadre for a little over a year. The Brotha's knew how I moved and respected my get down. They all also knew what I was going through with Carla. Hell, they even witnessed her decline. These were my brotha's. They stood by my side while I stood by hers.

We jumped in three cars and made our way to the 69 (six nine) Village for the meeting. The Village was grimy and deadly. They'd been like that since the days of Big Fee and the Village Mob. We pulled up and was greeted by a small army. We were Gaidi's (gah-ee-dee's), so we showed no fear of what was supposed to be intimidation.

The meeting lasted for over an hour, but it didn't go well. At one point I started to wonder if we would actually make it out of there. When the nigga that touched my baby walked in the room it took six brotha's to hold me down and keep me from killing him with my bare hands. The nigga lied and said he didn't know that Carla was my old lady. Everybody in the streets knew who Carla belonged to because I done had to put my foot in a couple of niggaz ass behind Carla and her crack habit.

In the end, there wasn't much that we could do. The Family didn't condone black-on-black punishment. Which meant members were not supposed to put their hands on each other. Their "C" told us that the nigga would be severely DP'd behind what had happened simply because he'd done what he did to a black woman. There was nothing extra about her being my woman or the fact that the mothafucka was selling dope. Shit, they all did it.

I left the meeting with one thing on my mind. I didn't give a fuck about laws, codes of conduct, or codes of Ethics. Which were the rules and laws that we abided by in The Family. I was going to kill him. I'd actually made that decision before the meeting. I made it that night while sitting on the couch holding Carla in my arms.

For the next couple of weeks, it was all about Carla. By now I was working on the construction. After talking to my boss and letting him know I had a family emergency, I took some time off work. I spent every single moment with her. It was a bittersweet time. It was the first time she'd gone that long without getting high since I'd come home. She opened up to me and cried her heart out. And I convinced her to try out one of the new drug rehab places that people were talking about. She agreed, promising me that she was tired. She said that she could feel the dope killing her. During that two-week period the two of us got closer than ever it seemed.

People were able to take a few personal items with them into rehab. Carla loved music. The rap and hip-hop scenes were really big, and Carla fell in love with it. She gave me a list of her favorites and I got her some tapes. The first two names on her list were Mc Hammer and Too Short. She also had Baby D, Del The Funky Homosapien, Digital Underground, The Hieroglyphics, and Young Blood. She also wrote some singers from Oakland on there too such as En Vogue, Oak Town 357, and Tony! Toni! Toné! with Raphael Saadiq, The Pointer Sisters, and Tower of Power. Oh yeah and Shelia E. repped Oakland like no other musician before her. She dated a big-time drug dealer named Holly Rock and made one of her biggest songs ever about him.

I went to the Eastmont Mall and found half the tapes that were on her list. The rest I picked up at The Durant Square, Oakland's own Flea Market. You could find damn near anything at the Durant. The day before she went into the program, we went to her mother's house to see you. We spent the entire day having fun. Carla and I didn't go to sleep that night. We stayed up all night talking and making plans about the future. We made love once and the next morning I took her to the program.

I was lost without her, even though I knew she needed the help. I hated myself for letting her go. The first couple of days I sat around moping. Then I decided to kick it into gear. I remembered hearing somewhere that a dope fiend often hid dope around the house to find on rainy days when they couldn't get some from anywhere else. I cleaned the house from top to bottom. Sure enough, I found hella shit; burned and used pipes, pieces of Brillo Pads, little bundles of crack rocks stashed behind boxes of cereal. It was crazy. I went over the house three times to make sure I didn't miss anything.

A couple of weeks later I decided to try and take my mind off of missing my Queen. There was a rap concert featuring all local Oakland and Bay Area groups. Everyone from Mc Pooh, Mc Hammer, 3X Krazy, Too Short and the Dangerous Crew, Totally Insane from East Palo Alto, Master P and TRU E-40 and the Click from Vallejo, Rappin' 4-Tay, and Ron C. Everybody was going to be there. A bunch of us decided to go to the concert.

The show was live! Everybody who was anybody was there. I remember seeing The East Bay Dragons. They were California's largest black motorcycle club with their headquarters right out of Oakland.

An old Comrade had started the East Bay Dragons. Members of damn near every click was there.

A major fight broke out. I don't know if it was on stage or behind the stage, but my attention had been drawn elsewhere. No more than fifteen or so feet away from me was the bitch as nigga that beat up Carla. I didn't hesitate to think about the consequences of my actions. I stormed over to him and socked him right in the jaw. It was on. Then a fight broke out between me and my comrades and him and the niggaz that were with him. People thought the fight from the stage had spilled out into the audience. People were running all over the place trying to get away from the melee. For a minute, it felt like I was back in the prison yard in the middle of a riot.

Bodies were literally flying through the air. Mothafuckas were getting stomped like O-Dog did that nigga in *Menace to Society*. In the midst of the confusion and chaos, I was stomping the shit out of the nigga. I don't know who was winning the fight between the two camps, but I was certainly fucking him up. I reached into my waist and pulled out my Glock 17 while he was on the ground. I shot him four times.

I was in violation of Family protocols, but I didn't give a fuck. Carla was my family. What about a husband's protocol? That was what was on my mind as I pulled the trigger. Chaos turned into pandemonium.

Simba rushed to my side yelling that we had to get the fuck outta dodge. A couple of niggaz were still trying to throw blows, but for the most part, everybody got the fuck up out of there. We made sure that we all made it back to the car before we drove off. Wasn't gone be none of that leaving mothafuckas behind shit.

No one said anything on the ride back to The Clubhouse about me violating rules by socking that nigga in the jaw. Everybody was too busy ranting and raving about how they were kicking the shit out of this person or that person. Me, I sat there silently thinking about Carla and the fact that I probably would never see her again. Putting your hands on another comrade was a no-no that was severely punished. Killing a comrade and it wasn't sanctioned was a death sentence. And I shot the nigga in front of the whole world to see.

CHAPTER 8

Oakland has been one of California's most violent and deadliest cities since the 80s. From the drug wars to the turf wars, it wasn't out of the ordinary to have over 100 murders a year. Most of the killings went down in East and West Oakland. North Oakland for the most part stayed away from the killing field.

That day at the concert, I never considered that my actions could possibly contribute to those numbers drastically, but they did. There was never a sit-down. No meeting to discuss what went down. Nothing. The tension between the old regime and the new regime had been building for so long. Both sides knew it was inevitable. The shit was going to hit the fan sooner or later. I just happened to be the spark that lit the fuse.

An all-out war erupted. See the thing about The Family or Jama (Jah-ma) is we are an organization of revolutionary soldiers from all over. Thus, we have members from various clicks all over. When this war erupted, we had niggaz from almost every turf in Oakland involved. Basically, the entire city was at war. Bodies were dropping like raindrops during a blizzard. The fact that so many comrades were from other turfs made things worst. Because their homes from the turf joined in on the war.

Word was sent down through The Central Committee, which is the governing body that controls The Family to end the war. By then there had been too much bloodshed. A simple cease-fire could not be had.

There were stories in The Oakland Tribune, the city's own newspaper, about new killings every day. Sometimes there were three or four different killings from multiple shootings the night before inside of the paper. My body count was climbing, and my name was buzzing in the streets.

When Carla came home from rehab, I was so happy. My baby looked like a new woman. In the rehab, she put on all the weight that she had lost from smoking. Plus, a little extra! She was thicker than all of them sistah's in En Vogue combined. Like the youngsters were saying nowadays. "She was thicker than a snicker."

We had longed for each other so bad while she was inside the rehab. We ended up locking ourselves in the house for a week straight when she got out. All we did was talk and make love. I'd missed my Baby so long, it felt like I had died and gone to Heaven.

When we finally surfaced it was to get something to eat. I told her we could go anywhere she wanted. There were a few places at The Jack London Square I thought she might choose. She surprised me by saying she wanted to go to the Quarter Pound Burger over on San Pablo Avenue.

It was about 8:00 p.m. when we drove the Cutlass over to the burger spot. Carla drove. She was excited when she found out that I had the car fixed up for her as a gift. I had it painted Candy Apple Grape with two white race stripes down the middle. The interior was cocaine white with Zeniths on hunnid spokes. In the trunk, it sounded like Godzilla and King Kong. She loved it.

Carla heard a little about the violence that had been going on in the streets. We talked about it, but I didn't go into detail. I shared the basics and left it at that.

Seagram's new tape *Reality Check* was bumping in the tape deck, he was spitting that fire. My eyes were on a swivel as we drove. Things got so crazy and hectic. I had to analyze and dissect everything that I saw. It was a nice crowd of people at the Quarter Pounder like always. It was the most popular burger spot in the town. I studied the group of people as Carla found a place to park. Looking for any face that was out of place or a set of eyes that didn't belong. A few heads turned our way due to the sound system. Yet the looks were those of admiration from some and envy from others who were mad they couldn't afford a system like that inside of their ride.

I didn't peep any potential threats. I climbed out of the car and left my Glock on the seat, while I went to go and place our order. I gave a head nod and threw a piece sign at a few of the dudes that I knew on my way to the window to place our order. The smell of the food was everywhere in the air wreaking havoc on a niggaz taste buds. The aroma was the strongest right in front of the ordering window. Sauteed mushrooms and onions along with the juicy thick slices of bacon mixed and danced off the smell of seasoned ground beef and melted cheese creating an aroma to die for.

When I finished placing our order. I was getting ready to turn around when an ice-cold, teeth-shattering chill ran up and down my spine. I knew the feeling; I've felt it many times before. It was that of danger. The Reaper was approaching my doorstep. I turned around anyway and was staring directly down the barrel of a .357 Bulldog. The face behind the gum belongs to the nigga that put his hands on my Carla. The nigga I'd stomped the shit out of and shot four times at the Luniz concert.

My first thought went to my Glock that I had left on the seat of the car. My next thought was I hope Carla wasn't looking. I wouldn't want her to have to live with the memory of witnessing a nigga kill me right in front of her. Who was I kidding, of course, she was looking. We were parked directly facing the front of the hamburger shack.

I didn't turn my head nor blink my eyes. I would greet death the same way that I greeted life, like a man. People started backing up and putting some distance between themselves and us. They were preparing to break wide when the opportunity presented itself.

Turns out he was one of them show-boating, loudmouth, talk too much ass niggaz. Instead of handling his business like a "G", he decided to put on a show for the crowd by talking shit. The last thing that I heard before the shots rang out was "Nigga you chose to say fuck yo life over a funky dope fiend bitch!"

Something crashed into my face at point-blank range just before I felt the wind of the first bullet flying by my face. Realization of what was popping off hit me in enough time to duck before the second bullet burrowed a hole in the space where my head just was at a split second ago. Then I heard her voice. "Not a dope fiend bitch, a real bitch! You bitch ass nigga!"

It was Carla, I was correct. She had peeped the move from inside of the Cutlass. When she saw the nigga stalking up to me from behind, she grabbed my Glock off of the seat and slipped out of the car. No one paid her any attention. Everybody was too busy paying attention to the loudmouth as he bumped his gums. This gave Carla enough time to sneak up behind the nigga. She put the Glock right up on the back of his head and squeezed the trigger just as he was completing his last sentence.

It was parts of his skull and brain matter that had smacked against my face before that first bullet flew by. Carla was so close to the nigga that the bullets penetrated his skull and blew the front of his face smooth the fuck off as they exited his head and kept flying.

As his lifeless body was crumbling to the ground pandemonium erupted. People went everywhere. It was like the concert all over again.

Looking past the body falling. I saw my baby standing there looking like ole' girl that said *Rock-a-bye Baby* in New Jack City. Right at that moment, my heart dropped completely out of my chest. Carla wasn't the only thing I was seeing. A police car was pulling into the parking lot right behind my baby. Everybody was running around like chickens with their heads off and here me and Carla was standing over a dead body with her holding the smoking gun.

I had to think fast, my baby had just gotten clean. In a sense, she had just gotten her life back. We couldn't make it to the Cutlass. The cop's Caprice was in front of it, blocking us from our only escape. I could break and run but that wouldn't solve the problem because I still had Carla and I didn't think a woman would outrun a cop. I did the only thing I could do, the only thing a real man would do.... I told her that I loved her more than life itself as I snatched the Glock out of her hand and squeezed off two more shots into the already dead body.

"Freeze!"

I never in my life thought I would be happy to hear that word. But I knew that to the cop, it looked like I killed the nigga laying on the ground. Even if he saw Carla holding the gun when he pulled into the parking lot, his new memory of me standing over the nigga squeezing the trigger would override the other memory and his conscious would tell him that it was me holding the gun when he first pulled in.

Carla was crying and begging me. I wasn't hearing it though. I wasn't about to let the woman I love spend one day in jail, let alone spend the rest of her life in prison. I had already been to prison. Already done prison time. I knew how to survive, but more importantly, I knew I would survive. I had a smile on my face and a warm feeling in my heart as the cop placed the handcuffs on my wrist. I was protecting my woman like a man is supposed to.

Even when I was sentenced to 50 to life. I still had that warm feeling in my heart as I looked in the back of the courtroom and saw Carla. Not a dope fiend bitch or real bitch. I chose to say fuck my life over my Queen!

Two months later I was inside of Badger Section at San Quentin State Penitentiary. When I was called to see the counselor. San Quentin was a level 2 prison at the time. It was also the reception center for Northern California. Badger Section is where they house convicts with higher security levels. I was a level 4. My counselor informed me once I got to her office that Carla's mom called to inform me that Carla was dead. She started getting high again shortly after I had gotten arrested. They found her inside the house. She'd been dead for over a week. She died from a heart attack which is common when you overdose on crack....

(Ty Dollar-Sign)

At first, I thought Pops had paused to think. When it seemed that his pause was longer than I figured it should have been. I looked up and across the table. I had never in my life seen Pops cry. Yet sitting across from me after telling me the story, he now sat silently crying. Mom's death must've really been hard on him if it's still affecting him now.

"Pops...." I began but he held his hand up and started shaking his head.

"I-I'm alright Ty. Aint nothing wrong with a man shedding a tear. Men get affected by things emotionally just like anybody else. And real men don't have a problem letting it show. I could hear the dignity in his voice as he spoke.

I didn't say anything else. I sat back and nodded my head at the truth in his words. I got up from the table. For one it felt like me witnessing him crying, that I was somehow intruding on something intimately. The second reason I got up was to fix us both a drink. He looked like he could use one and I knew damn well I did. By the time I got back to the table with a glass in each hand, he had fixed himself together and was just sitting there with a lost look in his eyes. I handed him his glass and walked back to my chair.

"Why didn't you tell me the truth a long time ago?" I finally asked him. I was tired of just sitting there. Plus, I felt he still owed me answers.

"It didn't really matter. You'd already hated me so much and blamed me for your mama's death. I didn't want you hating her too which is what would've happened if I had told you the truth. It was bad enough that you didn't have her. I wasn't going to take away your memory of her too."

"Maybe when I was younger, I could see that. But Pops I been old enough to separate the bullshit for a minute. You could've pulled my coat and kept it a hunnid with a nigga." I was pissed off a little bit. In reality a nigga was more hurt than anything.

All this time, Big Mama never would tell a nigga the details of how moms died. All she would tell me was it was my Pops fault. She used to say that Pops wasn't a no-good criminal that was always in and out of prison. After hearing that shit for so long it was only natural that I started believing that shit too. Especially on them lonely days when a nigga hated God for me not having a mother.

"Like I said wasn't no sense in making you hate your mother too. I couldn't sacrifice that little sense of peace you had just to try to gain favor and a way into your heart. I knew in time we would develop a relationship. Life is funny that way."

"Then why are you telling me now? What's the point of a last-minute confession?"

"Because it's important for you to know the truth."

"Why? What's so damn important now... I mean besides you dying?" I sounded like a little fucking seven-year-old child. I knew this but I couldn't help it.

"Because son, somebody's gotta break the cycle that we're stuck in. And I think you're strong enough to do it. You just needed the motivation. Hell, I believed the real truth would motivate you. Tyrone the truth is, I love you. I always loved you, just as much as I loved your mama. As black men, we don't hear those words enough. We hear a slew of negative and derogatory shit in our lives. Too much of it in fact. But we don't hear what's most important. That someone loves us. That we're actually good enough for someone to love us."

"I didn't share the truth with you so you would know that your mother was a drug addict or that she committed suicide. I needed you to know the truth behind why I went to prison. You gotta understand, first of all, I only had a split second to make the best decision for the future. All of our futures. And out of the three of us, your future was the most important. You would not have had a future being raised by an ex-convict who had openly declared war on drug dealers. Shit if I didn't get you killed. You would've somehow gotten mixed up in my bullshit. Plus, a child needs the love of his mother. When your mother came out of rehab, she had that spark back in her eye. The week we spent shacked up when she came home, she talked to me about so many things that she wanted to do, so many goals. I figured you had a better chance at a better upbringing with her than you did with me. I loved you enough to sacrifice my life in order to give you a chance in life. Not because you were Carla's child but because you were our child. A boy needs to know that he is loved. Especially a young black boy. But just as importantly a man needs to know that he is loved too."

CHAPTER 9

Pops was right. I needed to know that I was loved. All the anger that I'd felt, all of the violence I embraced, all the negative energy that surrounded me, was because all my life I felt like no one loved me. I thought my Pops didn't love me enough to stay out of prison and my mom didn't love me enough to stay alive. No one cared about me, so I didn't care.

It's been a year since Pops passed away. The doctors were wrong with their calculations of how long he had to live. He died two days after the day he finished telling me the truth. I wish we would've had a little more time. There was so much I wanted to tell him. Starting with letting him know that I forgive him. I couldn't tell him that right away because hell, I didn't even realize that I did forgive until like three months after he was already gone.

"I wish you were here Pops to get a chance to see that your sacrifice paid off fo shizzle. I'm taking classes at UC Santa Cruz, and I bumped into Angela Davis, she's a professor at the University. After I introduced myself and told her about moms and aunt Elaine, she welcomed me with open arms. I've learned so much about mom and the struggle of our people from her." I paused so I could sit down on the lawn with my back against the headstone. "Don't worry Pops, I'm not being recruited as a revolutionary. You don't have to worry about that. I'm helping our people in another way. See Pops I got a love for music like mom had. We got a nice little movement going right now in the Bay Area called the Hyphy Movement. Your homeboy DJ Daryl has been helping me home in my engineering skills. With the advice that I'm getting from him and the knowledge I'm getting from my engineering classes at the University, I've managed to create my own sound. It's a sound that everybody 's feeling Pop! Ya Boi is in high demand right now. I just finished some work for San Quinn and Mistah Fab. I'm finna do a project with Keak Da Sneak. He wants me to work with him and his homeboy PSD the Driver for this project called The Farm Boys. Anyway, Pop I gotta get up outta here. I just wanted to let you know that your Love does matter, and your sacrifice was for something. I ain't cut my ties with The Gas Nation yet but I'm working on something right now to handle that. I love you Pop." I cracked the top on the bottle of bourbon I had brought.

I stood up and poured the bottle out on top of the grave. My heart was heavy, but I had a smile on my face. I wish somehow, I could've went back in time. So, I would've had more time to spend with the man who loved me like I was his own child. But I was happy that he'd decided to keep it real with me. I had already spent time at mom's grave before coming over to Pops. Even still I walked back over to hers to say goodbye again. Now knowing the truth about her death, I felt a little closer to her. Somehow, I shared her pain with her. The pain of lonesomeness of not having the love of the person you yearn for there with you.

Becoming Xena

Written by
Danae Braggs

After several meetings, countless phone conversations, and what seemed like a billion texts, Xena realized that she's hella feeling Ahmad. Which is why she knew she had to leave him alone. Immediately.

My dad, Richard, was a preacher. Yep, I'm a PK (short for preacher's kid). Most of my time as a child was spent sitting in some church pew. I've seen it all...the good, the bad, and definitely the ugly. I'm a very positive person so let's focus on the good. The good, in this case, is Ahmad.

I met him at New Gethsemane Church of God in Christ on Roosevelt Avenue in Richmond, CA. His grandmother, Ms. Estelle was a member there. Ahmad would stay with her during the summer, during school breaks, and visit on holidays.

I don't know where Ms. Estelle lived but I do know that she was a long-time member and loved her church. She was a sweet lady who sang in the choir and was also known and loved for the fact that she could cook! Folks would be hella mad when they missed out on whatever dish she made for any church potluck, dinner, or function.

Ahmad was definitely a product of Ms. Estelle. He was a rich, caramel-colored cutie. Very polite and respectful. He would always be the first on his feet to help with any and everything.

One Sunday morning, as we were getting ready for church. My dad sat me and my sister Yara down and told us we wouldn't be going to New Gethsemane anymore. I didn't hear much else he said. I completely tuned him out. I was devastated. I wouldn't get to see Ms. Estelle anymore and definitely would miss Ahmad.

I had no idea why but at that same time we started church hopping. Needless to say, I lost contact with Ahmad. We moved several times around the Bay Area before eventually settling in Central Richmond. Yes, the infamous Iron Triangle.

Growing up in Central Richmond I saw a lot. Rival gang shootouts, retaliation, murders, dead bodies and not to mention the gun, drugs, and crooked cops. I started to become immune to it all. One of the craziest things that happened was finding out my dad was keeping a secret and watching this secret start to reveal itself about some shit my dad was into. Yeah, it seemed like my holy preacher dad was into some real money shit. Although he felt as though he was called by God to change his life for the better and to better lead his family, the niggas from his past didn't give a shit about any changes in him, his family, or the God he served. He was getting older, and I hated seeing him stress about whatever this shit was, the debt he owed behind it, and some things he had done to repay it. He was tired and at that point, I was old enough to do something about it.

My dad never let the two parts of his life cross paths. We looked and seemed like a normal little church-going family that lived in the hood.

Yara and I would always walk to La Perla and get a La Concha. It was soo good. Fried tortilla shell bowl, carne asada, ground beef, cheese, lettuce, sour cream. Mine was always the same every single time.

One day as we were walking back home, we saw a white Mercedes-Benz speed off from in front of our house. Yara and I both saw that there was a gold emblem on the back of the car, but I couldn't really make out what it was. As soon as that car was out of sight, we ran in the house to find our father sitting at the kitchen table with his head in his palms. He was mad as hell. Yara and I just stood there in silence. We had never really seen him like that before.

Without even looking at us he said with a stern voice "Don't y'all dare speak a word of what y'all saw to your mother." My mom, Christine, was a strong black woman who took no shit and was always there to help.

She worked as a nurse at nearby Kaiser Hospital. A couple of hours later mom came home. Dad gave no signs that anything was wrong, and we didn't either. We didn't say a thing. I hated this for my dad. I knew I had to do something.

Living in the heart of the Iron Triangle I met people from all walks of life, but nothing kept my attention like a nigga getting money. One, in particular, was a guy by the name of Onyx. I met him just before my 18th birthday on a beautiful summer day. The weather wasn't too hot, everything was just right.

I was walking down Barrett on my way to the liquor store, and he pulled up on me in a clean-ass Cutlass. Emerald green candy paint on Dayton's and Vogues with all the boom in the trunk. He rolled down the window and politely asked my name. I told him, Xena, with an X. He told me I was beautiful and asked if he could call me. I shyly replied thank you and gave him my number. He asked if I was going far. I said no, just right here to the store then back home. His phone rang. He said he had to get to work and told me to be safe out here and get back home.

Onyx was fine! The dark brown complexion and slim build seemed tall even though he was sitting in the car, with a perfect smile and a dimple in the lower part of his right cheek. Fresh haircut, faded. He was fitted from head to toe. I could tell this was about to be the beginning of some real-life Bonnie and Clyde shit.

Onyx called later that night and we talked for a long time. He was very intelligent and didn't seem like some of these other hood ass niggas that repeatedly try to holla especially knowing my dad is a preacher. You know what they think and say about the preacher's daughter.

A few days later Onyx called and asked if I wanted to go get something to eat. Of course, I said yes, let's go to Portumex. He was like ok cool; I'll be there in a few minutes.

I was listening real hard for the boom in his car getting closer. I looked out the window and saw that green candy paint pull up. I told Yara I would be back but not much else. I figured the less she knew the less she would have to lie if questioned by our parents.

I quietly tipped out the front door and jumped in the car. It was a nice warm day. I rolled my window down and let the sunshine on my face as we made our way up Barrett Ave to 23rd St. Portumex is a quaint little family-owned restaurant that had been there for years.

Onyx was enamored with the damn fish tacos but couldn't quite decide, I already knew what I wanted. I always got the same shit. Chicken enchilada dinner plate with the house sauce on my side salad and for my chips and salsa. I guess I'm a creature of habit. We talked as we waited for our food to be served.

I didn't really hear what he was saying. Onyx was so fine I got lost in his words. I glanced around the restaurant and brought my eyes back to his smooth brown skin. He smiled and said "I want to spend the whole day with you. What you wanna do after this?" I looked up at the ceiling and told him I had no idea. He put his hand on mine and asked me if I was sure I wanted to kick it with him today. I said absolutely! He told me to think about what I wanted to do while we eat. We finished and made our way back to his car. He said "Well, we can't just sit here". I figured I would test the waters and I was like ok let's go to Great America. Great America is an amusement park about an hour away from Richmond if there is minimal traffic which was hardly ever. There's always traffic in the Bay Area. He was like cool, let's do it!

We made it through traffic and had a blast at Great America. We got back to Richmond just before my mom's shift was over at the hospital. I called and checked with Yara to make sure it was clear to come in. I made it to my room just before I heard my mom's keys in the door. Shit that was close.

The next day I was sitting outside, and Onyx pulled up. He asked if I wanted to make a run with him real quick. I said "Duh!" Like I would say no. Of course, I did. I wanted to be anywhere he was. I felt safe with him. I hopped in the car, no questions asked.

We ended up in Oakland. East Oakland to be exact and met up with his cousin Rico. Rico was on the move and needed to head out fast, so Onyx shook his hand, grabbed a Gucci duffle bag from him, and tossed it in the trunk. We headed back to Richmond. On the way back we talked about a lot of things but mostly money. At one point in the conversation, things took a turn, and sadness came over me. He asked me what was wrong. I couldn't help but tell him some of what was bothering me, but I couldn't tell him everything yet. All I could say was that my dad seemed to be having some money trouble and I've been trying to figure out a way to help him.

Onyx had to make a stop and handle some business, so he dropped me off at home. I walked in the front door and the how house was dark except for the light coming from under the door of my parent's bedroom. My mom wasn't home from work, but I could hear my dad talking. He was praying. Now, I've heard my dad pray before, but this time was different. He sounded scared and defeated. I couldn't hear exactly what he was saying but I knew it had to do with the money he owed someone. I was still standing there when I heard my mom's keys jingling as she was trying to unlock the front door. As I took a step to walk away towards my room, I overheard my dad mention the name "King". It was time for me to do something.

One week later I turned 18. My parents threw me a big birthday party. This was the day that I introduced Onyx to my mom and dad. I was terrified that they would hate him and judge him with their "extra Christian eyes". They didn't hate him. They actually loved him. My dad was especially impressed and said that Onyx reminded him of himself when he was younger. I'm so glad they were cool because I was in love with him.

After the party, Onyx and I went for a night ride. We found a nice place to park where we could get out and look at the stars. We talked about what the future looked like for us together and individually. He wanted to be with me, and I wanted to be with him no matter what. Point, blank, period. He was gazing at me, and I felt so connected to him. It was deep. We sat there and talked for what seemed like hours. Then his phone rang. It was Rico.

Onyx didn't say much. He mostly listened as if he was getting some kind of instructions. Rico gave him some more information and asked if he had the "key" on him. Onyx told him it was at the house. Rico said, "cool, let me know when you grab it". Onyx said, "I'm chillin' with Boss Lady right now. Imma hit you in a minute" and hung up the phone. He looked over at me. I had a slightly confused look on my face. All I could say was "boss lady?" He said, "hell yeah, we are about to go big and you're the boss!" Then he handed me a small rectangular box... the kind you get from a jewelry store. The box was red velvet, soft to the touch, with gold lettering on it. "Open it," Onyx said. I pulled off the top of the box and inside was a 24-karat gold necklace with a 24-karat gold pendant completely covered in diamonds that said, "BOSS LADY". All I could say was "Oh my GOD! Thank you!" He said, "You're welcome and Happy Birthday!" Then he asked if I was ready to go home. I said, "no, let's go to yours."

Onyx had a nice 2 bedroom, 2 bath apartment near Hilltop. As we walked in the front door, I noticed he or whoever furnished this apartment had really good taste. I could barely see what was around me, because I had tunnel vision with my sights on his bedroom door. He asked if I wanted anything to eat or drink. I told him no thank you as I stared at him. He said, "Ok, turn around."

He grabbed the jewelry box from my hand and took the necklace out. He gently moved my just past shoulder-length hair off to the side.

Then he placed the necklace around my neck and locked the clasp. Onyx wrapped his arms around me from behind and kissed me on the back of my neck. His hands moved over my stomach, across my breasts, then back down to my hips. He turned me around and looked into my eyes. I could feel him get hard. No words needed to be said. We both knew what was about to happen.

He took my hand and led me down the hallway to his room. He opened the door, and we walked in slowly. He laid me on his bed. My heart was racing. I started thinking "what if something happened?" I was more nervous now than any of the times we took those "rides" over the last couple of months. Half a second later all the fear and anxiety was gone with one gentle kiss. At that moment I didn't care about anything else in the world except what was about to happen in that bedroom. He undressed me. It seemed like we were both moving in slow motion, and it felt like my clothes just melted off. To be honest I don't remember taking anything off, helping or moving, etc. That was all him. I was definitely caught up in the moment. I laid back on the bed and laid on top of me. He rubbed his hands up inner my thighs then under my ass. He pushed my legs back and pushed his dick inside me. I felt every inch of him. Oh my GOD! This wasn't the first time, and he wasn't the first guy, but it was the first time with him, and he was the best by far. Damn, I'm in love!

I woke up to the sun shining on my face. It was a warm and relaxing feeling. I felt amazing and smelled bacon. This nigga cooks too!??! I hit the muthafuckin jackpot! He was about his money; his Boss Lady and he could cook. Onyx walked into the room with a tray. Orange juice, an omelet, bacon, sausage, and toast. It was beautiful. He told me to eat while he hopped in the shower. I took a few bites and couldn't help but jump in the shower with him. On my way to the bathroom, I noticed a partially unzipped duffle bag slightly sticking out of the closet. All I could see was money, but I wasn't concerned with that. That's what we did... get money! After our shower, we got dressed and Onyx asked if I was working today. "Of course,", I said. "Alright, all we gotta do is drop this "key" in San Jose", Onyx explained. "That's cool with me", I replied. So far, I already had about $32,000 in a lock box from the last few runs we had gone on.

We headed out to San Jose. It was another nice, warm, sunny day. The music in the car was blasting while the wind was blowing through my hair. Onyx looked over at me and said, "You know I would never let anything, or anyone hurt you, right?" "Yeah, I know" I replied. I looked at him and I looked into his eyes. I could tell he meant what he said. Everything was perfect and I felt amazing. I made up my mind right then and there to step into who I was born to be... Boss Lady!

Onyx and I made it to our destination. We got out of the car looking like we hopped straight off of a magazine cover. My necklace was blinging and glistening in the sun. We made our way to the side door of this dull grey warehouse and walked in. I had the "key" in my hand. I looked down at it and noticed it was engraved with a small gold crown that had a red heart in the middle of it. I know I have seen that logo before but couldn't remember where.

We made our way down this long, dark hallway where we were met by a guard. He was big, Black, and ugly. He looked like he had been in the penitentiary for a while recently. This dude had what I call "prison muscles". Just huge for no damn reason and his face looked like he had been beaten with an ugly stick. Just ugly. He stood there with a hard mean mug and his arms semi-folded. As we got closer, I heard him say "this way".

We followed him around a corner and then through these huge, metal double doors. As we walked in, I looked around and saw an older Black man standing near a shelf. He was very tall. I noticed a machine on the desk. I couldn't tell exactly what it was, but the man told me to put the key in the slot. He said, "If the key starts the machine, we're all good." I put the key in and stepped back. The man looked at my necklace and said, "Boss Lady, huh?" I nodded my head yes and he gave a semi-half-smirk smile. Strange.

Anyway, the machine started, and the man seemed pleased with the outcome. Without saying a word, he handed Onyx an all-black leather duffle bag and walked away. Cha-ching! The big bodyguard dude led us back out the double doors, around the corner, and down the long hallway. He opened the door that led to the parking area for us and said, "y'all be easy!" Then he turned and walked away. The job was completed. We hopped in the car, looked at each other, and busted out laughing. That was probably the strangest job we had done so far.

We made it back to Richmond just as the sun was going down. Onyx made a right turn onto my street and as we came around the corner, we could see flashing lights. There was an ambulance there and police cars everywhere. What the hell was going on? Onyx parked a few houses down. We jumped out of the car and ran towards my house. All of the neighbors were standing outside watching. I saw Yara sitting on our next-door neighbor's porch. She had her head down in her hands and she was crying. I ran up to her and asked, "what was happening?"

She continued to cry then screamed, "Daddy is dead!". Onyx and I calmed Yara down and walked her to his car. Through my tears, I managed to ask Yara to tell us exactly what happened. She said she wasn't completely sure, but she heard Daddy arguing with another man in the kitchen. All she could really remember was hearing some kind of scuffling and then Daddy saying "King don't do this! I just need a little more time!" Then the man said, "No more time! Your time is up!" Then there were two gunshots. The man walked out the front door.

I asked her if she had already talked to the police, and she said no. Onyx told her to say as little as possible to the police and anyone else for that matter. He said "Do not give them the name or any other details. All you need to say is you heard men arguing and then gunshots". Yara understood what Onyx was telling her and agreed to do what he said.

A few minutes later my mom's car pulled up. She frantically jumped out of the car after barely putting it in the park. Mom screamed, "Richard, Xena, Yara!!!" As she made her way under the yellow caution tape and an officer stopped her before she got to the front door. I felt terrible. My mom and sister are inconsolable. I knew as soon as Yara said Daddy is dead that his secret life and money problem had caught up with him. I made a promise to myself at that very moment that I wouldn't rest until I found "King" and made him pay for what he had done to my father and my family.

Fast Forward

For the last three years, I have dedicated my life to building an empire and finding the guy that murdered my dad. I'm a 21-year-old boss! I got the money, the power, the respect, and the man. I got my real estate license and started a successful real estate business as well as an interior design and staging company. I brought Yara in as my assistant and focused on buying investment properties and then renting them out. Yes, these were business dreams of mine but also a great way to move all this cash around. Onyx and I were no longer doing runs regularly. We made so much money doing them that we had to figure out what to do with it. We needed some way to make it legal.

It's a gloomy Monday in March. I'm already not feeling it. Yara had scheduled a showing appointment for a listing that I have in Pinole for 10 am. I feel like shit. The day feels weird already, but I get in my coke white Mercedes Benz S65 AMG, turn the music up, and hit I-80. I made it to Pinole in a few minutes and took the Appian Way exit. The neighborhood was very bright and familiar. I made my way to the house and go in. I turned on the lights and heater because it was cold and seemed hollow and echo-y. I opened the blinds and curtains as well to make it look more like a home instead of just some old house.

At 10 o'clock on the dot, the doorbell rang. I opened the door to find the beautiful black man. He was tall with a medium build and a caramel complexion. He said hello and extended his right hand to shake mine. "Good morning, my name is A.D.," he said. I couldn't put my finger on it but for some reason, this man looked hella familiar. I responded, "I'm Xena with an X. Nice to meet you A.D." He smiled and said, "Nice to meet you as well."

I noticed the look on his face change as if he realized something. I invited him in and we started the tour of the house. He told me a little about the trucking business he owned. A.D. was very articulate, well-spoken, and smelled amazing. I reminded myself that this is business but now I'm captivated because I really feel like I know him. A few minutes later we finished the tour of the house. "I love this house", said A.D. "And I would like to put an offer in on it... all cash." I smiled professionally and said "ok, I'll write it up and call you at 2 pm to discuss it." I locked up the house and he walked me to my car.

He told me he was looking into purchasing several properties and would like to work with me exclusively. I said, "That would be great and I'm looking forward to working with you". I got in my car, and he walked to his then drove off. I noticed a small emblem on the back of his car. It was a gold heart with a heart in the middle. I sat there for a few seconds thinking about this strange feeling I had and how familiar this guy was. I decided to go to my office to work on his offer.

I walked into my office and talked to Yara. I asked her about A.D and if he was a referral. She said a man called and said his nephew was interested in that house in Pinole. He gave the name A.D. and asked for an appointment. That was pretty much it. I told her that A.D. seemed really familiar to me, and he wanted to work with me exclusively on several property purchases. "That sounds amazing!" Yara said. I told her he wanted to put an all-cash offer on the Pinole house and chat with me at 2 o'clock. "Okkkkk!" Yara yelled, "Get it, Boss Lady!"

At 2 o'clock I called A.D. We discussed his offer and decided to send it to the sellers immediately after our phone call. Then A.D. told me something that threw me for a loop. He said, "I remember you". I said, "You do?" He said "Yes... New Gethsemane!" All I could say was "Whaaaaaaaat???? Ahmad?????"

He said, "Yes, it's me!"

Ahmad explained that his uncle was some high-profile rich dude, and he handled a lot of business for him as he is getting older. This was crazy. He said the moment I introduced myself as Xena with an X he knew it was me. I told him that I had a weird feeling about today and when we met at the house, he seemed familiar. I just couldn't place where I knew him from or if I even knew him at all.

We spent some time getting caught up on what has been going on with each of us for about the last 10 years or so. He told me that his grandmother, Ms. Estelle, had passed away about 5 years ago. I gave him my condolences and told him about my dad passing away 3 years ago. He told me how sorry he was to hear that and that he had always admired my dad.

Ahmad asked how my mom and Yara were doing, and I told him they were doing well. "My mom is still working at the hospital and Yara is now my assistant", I explained. He said, "Ok! Y'all are killing it!" "We're trying!" I responded. I asked him if he was available to meet later in the week to go over budgets and price points, etc. for the properties he wanted to purchase. "I'm always available for you Xena with an X", he said.

He said he would text me his business card as soon as we hung up. I said, "Ok cool, either I or Yara will call you tomorrow to set our appointment. "Have a good evening, Xena" he said and hung up. Two seconds later I got the text of his business card. It read King's Legacy, LLC. Ahmad Denton – Owner. It was all black with gold lettering and the logo was a gold crown with a heart in the middle!!! Wait a minute!!!

The same logo on the back of his car and the same logo I remember seeing 3 years ago on that key Onyx and I dropped off in San Jose. I cannot tell Onyx or anyone else about this! I'll have to put this all together on my own. I need to find out who King is and how Ahmad is connected to him! Getting that information will be the key to finding out why my dad was killed.

To be continued...

San Francisco

Written by
Lyrics Brown

Intro
The City

S AN FRANCISCO THE HOME OF the Giants, Forty-Niners, and the Golden State Warriors. Home of the most crooked street in San Francisco, on Lombard Street, as well as Fisherman's Wharf, and Coit Tower. From cable cars to Twin Peaks, where you can look over the entire city. San Francisco is one of the most diverse places in the world.

The city's rich history goes back to a time when the Fillmore district was considered the Harlem of the West, for bringing some of the jazz world's elite to the area. Artists like Lionel Hampton, Charlie Parker, John Coltrane, Dizzy Gillespie, Miles Davis, and a plethora of others all came to the Fillmore District to swing out and be heard. As far back as the 1940s and '50s, if jazz was your thing, the Fillmore District was the place to be.

The world-famous Market Street runs from the Embarcadero all the way through the Castro district, where the LGBTQ community laid its roots.

San Francisco is also the home of many nationalities; the city has every culture that you can imagine. Throughout the city you can find just about every kind of food there is, from Chinese, Jamaican, Cuban, Thai, and a list of others.

The Mission district, as well as Chinatown, offer up a variety of events that definitely enhance your experience of San Francisco. From one part of the city to the next you could travel via Cable car to view all that the city has to offer you.

The North Beach area plays as your background as you site see traveling into the Pier 39 area of the city. After that, you can see the Downtown area as the energy of business getting handled as well as street performers captivating your mind with their alluring performances.

Popular venues such as the Warfield Theater, Bill Graham Civic Auditorium, and the Fillmore, host some of music's top acts in the world. Right in the heart of the Fillmore district, you can also find City Hall, home of mayor London Breed, who herself is from the Fillmore. Golden Gate Park is another well-known place in the city where you can find the Young Museum, the Japanese Tea Garden the California Academy of Science, and the San Francisco Botanical Garden.

When it comes to adventures, the city doesn't lack in that department. You could head down to Ocean Beach, where you could experience the Cliff House, one of the first arcade spots in the Bay Area. Another area of San Francisco that has a rich history is the Hunter's Point area. Home of Candlestick Park, where the Giants originally played, is the backdrop of this family-oriented community.

Places like the Bayview Opera House serve as a meeting place for kids and adults alike. The famous Third street leads to various neighborhoods such as Lakeview, Sunnydale, as well as the Mission district. The business also known as Muni connects people everywhere throughout the city. No matter what time it is you can always depend on Muni to be running.

As much beauty as there is in San Francisco, there is also a very ugly side to the city. Areas such as the Tenderloin district serves as a drug-invested playground for the less fortunate. Cocaine, Heroin, Meth, and anything else that you want, or need is at your disposal. Night walkers during the daytime parade their offerings in the hope of finding their next payday. Grimy eyes clock the purses of the unknowing as the Tenderloin streets bring out the worst of the worse.

You can't talk about the joy without talking about the pain, this being said leads us to the nightlife of San Francisco. Once the sun goes down the city comes all the way alive. The desire to feel good becomes high that most night owls are chasing. Places like the Power Exchange, allow you to unleash your inner freak as they say. Bronze Party, and Twist, also serve as the places you go to get your groove on.

Whatever your scene is, the city has it, rather you're the squarest of the square, or you're all the way about that wildlife, you can partake in it no matter what it is. These are just some of the things that make San Francisco go, like any big city you have your good and your bad, your triumphs and your disappointments, from the hippies on Haight Street to the Black Panthers who marched up and down the Fillmore streets. Fog city as it is sometimes known is one of the most interesting cities on the map.

Outside of breeding championship teams and developing some of today's top media platforms, San Francisco is and will always be known for the Golden Gate Bridge, Alcatraz, and the Loma Prieta earthquake in 1989.

Actors and Actresses, such as Danielle Steel, Danny Glover, Whoopie Goldberg, and Robin Williams, all hail from San Francisco.

In the world of sports San Francisco, has also had some of the best to ever do it. Such names as Jerry Rice, Joe Montana, Steph Curry, Ronnie Lott, and plenty of others have felt what it's like to be a champion.

Being from the city is a badge of honor that people wear proudly and securely, it's the way we walk, the way we talk, and most definitely the way we move throughout life.

Words like Woo Coo, YEE, Slaps, Juiced, Outta Pocket, and Hella, are words that you will hear on any given day in the city. From the way we dance to the way we hustle is simply the Bayway of doing things. Originality keeps the city at the forefront of setting trends, cities all over have taken a page from the San Francisco playbook.

Rather it be a cold foggy day, or the sun beaming causing the city to illuminate, San Francisco will forever be home. Outside of the major parts of the city, spots like Diamond Heights, and The Avenues, are gems that have something different to offer you while traveling throughout this diverse city.

If it's the retro feel that you are attracted to, the Haight Street district will supply you with all that you are looking for. Top restaurants, as well as hobby stores, fill the district making the Haight area one of the most visited areas in the Bay. You can find the original Ben and Jerry's ice cream store still in the place it began in, tattoo shops with fly little clothing stores lace the blocks of the Haight, giving you a taste of the old mixed with the new.

Haight Street is also known for 420 days, the day weed smokers from all over come to Hippie hill to partake in some of the finest buds that the city has to offer. This is a celebrated event that has been taking place for years and hopefully will continue being a part of the San Francisco experience for many more.

With so much history here in the Bay Area, San Francisco has and will forever be on people to visit list. The mystery of the city comes with many stories. If you ask anyone who is originally from San Francisco, if they would trade it for anything, I'm willing to bet that the answer would be a direct no. Even though there are beautiful cities throughout the world, none come with such a background that attracts old and young people in search of their freedom like San Francisco.

Families of every nationality come to the city to achieve the American dream, and the city is definitely the auditioning platform for survival on any level. If you can make it out here with the unexpected rain, the thick fog, and hot days that appear as if it's summertime, then you can guarantee that you can achieve your goals anywhere you plan on laying your roots down.

The sucka free as the youngsters call it will forever be the city that breeds leaders, entrepreneurs, and future millionaires alike. It's like the song goes, I left my heart in San Francisco and there's no place like home.

Chapter 1
Sideways

"Game recognizes game in the Bay main" JT the Bigger Figure slapped through the speakers as I got ready for work. This song was a staple in my upbringing and the fact JT was from Fillmore, made it that much better. It was a certain swag that came with being from the city, and it didn't matter what part you were from. If you lived in San Francisco, you had this energy that made you stand out.

From the infamous, The Catch by Dwight Clark, in 1982, to the Warrior's championship runs in 2015, 2017, and 2018. Being able to say that you were from the Bay Area was really something special, especially if you were born here, it solidified your authenticity as a real deal Baydestrian.

Being talented is an understatement when it comes to the city. Athletes, Singers, Rappers, philanthropists, and every kind of skill set that you could think of, all cohabitated in this melting pot that we call Frisco.

I live in the Fillmore district; we have our own style and way of doing shit. Most of my guys hustled for a living, but my one partner named Kenyon was definitely on his own page. While the rest of us kicked it on the block watching out for one time anyone studied into the wee hours of the morning preparing for his EMT exam. Ever since he was youngin all Kenyon wanted to do was be an EMT tech.

We used to clown him all the time telling him that he wasn't going to make it, but that just motivated him to stay at the top of his classes. Right out of high school Kenyon landed a job at Kaiser on Geary Street. He was getting his bread on in the realest way. The rest of us were still hustling to get our cake on as well. Darhino, Mayne, and Pudge were my boys.

We all grew up in Fillmore and have been knowing each other for over fifteen years now. Kenyon was our boy also; he was just moving to a different rhythm. They call me At It, but my government name is Alzir, I picked up my nickname after my folks Mayne, said that I'm always at it, meaning that I'm always at the money. When we were younger, we all told ourselves that we were not going to be living check to check ever.

This was something that I made sure I stayed on top of. Not having money was like not having air to breathe, and we all know you need air. That's how I looked at money, it was always something that I knew would get me to the next level in life. Even though Kenyon had chosen to walk the straight and narrow, he was still down with us.

Most Saturday nights you could find all of us chilling at Hawthorn club on Geary Street, this was our spot where we kicked it and conducted business. Now that we were all in our twenties we definitely moved with more precaution. The vibe was always solid when we came around, we had acquired a reputation for being the ones that you didn't ask too many questions about.

Like most crews, we had our fair share of haters who constantly tried to throw shade on our name, but the same way a cat is irrelevant to a do is the same way we felt about these clown-ass dudes. We had bigger things to be focusing on, Pudge had a plug down in Silicon Valley who was looking to get his hands on some pills. He was looking to spend up to five to ten thousand based on what we could get. He was into Oxycodone, plus he played with his nose from time to time.

Mykola Kushnir was this wild Ukrainian dude who Pudge met when he kicked it with his cousins down in Jersey. They hit it off having a common attraction to strippers, Mykola would shut whole clubs down just to watch certain dancers do their thing. Pudge just loved the dancers; he didn't care what body type they had as long as they let him fuck every now and then. After developing a rapport with Mykola, Pudge discovered that he was plugged into the heroin game real heavy. The only thing was, that he didn't work in the family business. He was the black sheep of his family and swore that he would never go back to his father for anything.

The story goes, Mykola used to have a problem with lady heroin, once his father found out about his issue, he had him committed to a rehabilitation center. That shit lasted all of three months before Mykola found a way to bust out from the facility. At that point, his father cut him out of the family business for good until he could get his shit together.

Unable to do right on a consistent basis led Mykola to get out of Jersey and never look back. He wound up meeting his lady who lived in California, and the rest as they say is history.

Mykola found himself in Silicon Valley turning the geeks onto a higher way of living, literally. Taking what he learned from Jersey, Mykola got it popping making a name for himself as the go-to man. Once he got everything set up in motion, he reached out to Pudge, and we have been rocking with him ever since. Pudge knew Mykola was good for the money, so he made sure to link up with Kenyon to get the good shit. Yeah, Kenyon was our plug for those hard-to-get pills.

He'd been swinging so much dick between three different hospitals to where he had all the plug on the goodies. Our shit was running like a well-oiled train on the track, we were getting that long dough from several different outlets throughout the city. We all were hungry being in our early twenties and by the looks of things we would be able to retire in our early forties if shit keeps on hitting like it was.

I had been staying on my own ever since I turned eighteen, now, Pudge and Darhino all lived together. I didn't know any other way. I lost both my parents at an early age, so I learned about things kind of differently when you talk about having both parents around to shape and mold your future. Nevertheless, being from the city taught me to be resilient in all that you do.

So, for me, I promised myself that I would never have to struggle for anything. This plug that we had with Mykola was going to be our introduction to the pill game. It was becoming the new thing on the block, Molly, Hydrocodone, and Percocet were the drugs of choice used by some of the top CEOs in the Bay Area. We were revolutionizing the pill game and taking it to places that it has never been before.

Kenyon was able to get his hands on multiple pills, we were looking to make at least ten stacks on this one deal. Pudge let us know that we were going to drop off the goods at Mykola in about an hour. Since I had a little time, I reached out to this chic I met last week at the Moxy, in Oakland.

"Hey, how have you been this Alzir? What's good wit you?" Karmai replied that she was cool.

"I'm glad you reached out. I was thinking about you." I found myself a little stuck as Karmai continued to talk.

"Yeah, I was thinking about our conversation that we had at Moxy. I was wondering if you were full of shit or not." We both bust out laughing. Karmai was on her shit over the phone, but I wanted to see how she handled herself in person.

"So, I'm thinking we should meet up so I can show you that I'm for real about mine." Karmai giggled before telling me that we could hook up later this evening if I didn't have any plans. I thought about it real quick before letting Karmai know that I was down to see her later on.

Now that I had that on lock, I focused on this meeting with Mykola. Dude could be a different beast if he's off too many pills, so we didn't know which version of him we would get. Mayne wasn't going to be making this run with us, he had some personal shit to handle, neither was Darhino who was out of town in Phoenix taking care of some new moves, so it was just me and Pudge on this trip.

Keeping it fair for everyone, we decided to meet in Palo Alto. This way, neither one of us had to travel too far. To date, we have never had any issues with Mykola, but just in case, both Pudge and myself had our poles with us. At the last minute, Mykola changed the meeting place to the Dumphy Hotel in San Mateo. Pudge didn't let the change of venues bother him; on the other hand, I instantly saw red flags go up.

"What's wrong folks?" Pudge asked, sounding concerned. I told him that I wasn't feeling the last-minute change made and that this shit didn't feel right to me. Although my gut was telling me to walk away from this shit, Pudge was all in and wanted to get this bread. Against my better judgment, I allowed myself to stick to the script. We were around ten minutes away when my phone started blowing up,

"Hello," on the other end of the phone was Mayne; he sounded stressed the fuck out.

"At it, I fucked up, bruh. I made a side deal with these motherfuckers, and now they are holding me up at this Self Storage spot on Mission Street; they talking about putting me into one of these storage units, bruh. Aww, shit, bruh!"

BOOM, BOOM, BOOM. What sounded like a cannon came loud and clear through the phone causing my ears to ring. Mayne's voice was no longer present as the silence confirmed that he was gone. With my ear still to the phone, I listened for any sign of what the fuck was going on. Right as I was about to hang up a voice whispered on the other end, "Even amongst a group of angels you will always find a demon." The voice was gone and my heart started beating like a college drumline.

"Pudge, get the fuck from over here NOW!" confused as to why I was tripping, Pudge didn't say a word; instead, he smashed away from the spot where we were supposed to be meeting Mykola at. Once we were like three blocks away, Pudge pulled over. "Bruh, what the fuck was that about?" Before telling him about Mayne, I took a deep breath.

"Bruh, that phone call was Mayne." A hard swallow followed before I revealed the unreal to Pudge. Tears ran down Pudge's face as the reality of what I was telling him to set in. This whole situation had gone to a place that I never could have imagined. I started thinking about what Mayne said as far as having a side deal, I had to find out what was the play on that in order to find out what went wrong. Totally oblivious, I forgot all about our deal with Mykola, I knew that he was going to be tripping off of our sudden decision to not show up.

After filling Pudge completely in on everything that went down, he was lost for words. His facial expression was one of hurt and anger all in one. I needed to talk to someone who had a cooler head than me, so I hit up Kenyon. After telling him everything Kenyon's exact words were, "This shit can't be real blood." No more words were exchanged as the silence became the soundtrack of the moment.

Chapter 2
City Situations

Back at the house, we all were in quiet mode. Kenyon was taking this shit hard as fuck, him being the rational one out of the crew had him feeling responsible for what happened to Mayne.

"We should have never been in this shit bruh, Mayne would still be here if we never would have got into this bullshit." Although Kenyon was right, there was nothing that we could do about it now. Pudge was going through it as well as he let out a loud holler,

"FUCK!" Pudge was hurt like we all were, Mayne was our boy and this shit had us fucked up in the realest way. Tired was an understatement as we all finally were able to get some long overdue rest. My rest was short-lived as my phone began buzzing like bees.

"Hello, who is this?" I answered somewhat irritated.

"This is Mykola, what the fuck happened to you guys, you just left me out there with nothing"

I really couldn't say anything that would make this right, so I decided to tell Mykola the truth about what happened to us. The reaction that Mykola gave wasn't one that I was expecting. He told me that he kind of already knew about the situation with Mayne, even though he wasn't still connected to his father's legacy. Mykola still had some loyal soldiers in the Ukrainian mafia who kept him updated on the latest and greatest when it came to the underworld's next big moves.

He went on to say that he heard Mayne was able to do a side deal with Yakiv Melnyk, who was the son of Anton Melnyk, who was a highly respected boss from Morgan Hill, which was a part of Silicon Valley. These dudes were playing with Crypto and other Bitcoin outlets, this pill shit was just another way for them to make some money. On the flip side, these same dudes would kill you in a heartbeat, the Melnyk family had a serious reputation for being heartless for real.

They were into that old-school way of punishing a motherfucker for doing them wrong, so I knew they tortured Mayne. I couldn't wait for Darhino to get back into town, he was our muscle, and most people didn't want to fuck with him. D, as we call him, was around 6-5 in height and weighed around 275 pounds in weight. His bald head and massive arms intimidated those who weren't as secure as he was.

He was known for having hands when it came to fighting, but these guns were Darhino's thing, and he was good at it. He knew about all kinds of weapons, especially guns though, we were going to have to bring everything we had in order to knock off the Melnyk family. One wrong move and the whole shit will go up in flames. I had to throw up my Do not disturb sign as my eyes could no longer fight the urge to close.

The sun wasn't playing fair at all, as the sun rays hit upon my window welcoming in another day. I could barely move due to the pain that my mind was going through. All night I thought about Mayne. I knew that he was always trying to get his bread up, but I never knew about his dealings with Yakiv. If I would have known there is no way that Mayne would have been dealing with the Melnyk family, those motherfuckers couldn't be trusted for nothing.

Darhino was scheduled to arrive back in the Bay Area today at 12:30 pm, there were so many things that I needed to tell him, I knew once he received the info about Mayne shit was going to go left. Having a couple of hours to kill before I went to pick D up, I reached out to Karmai. She had been on my mind, and I wanted to see if she was really about that life. I needed to change the narrative before I was right back in war mode. Before I hit her up, I hopped in the shower and got fresh. I didn't want to waste any time just in case she was with the foolery. After getting out of the shower I called up Karmai,

"Hey what's good love?" Karmai instantly started talking shit.

"Oh, now you have time for a bitch huh?" I couldn't help but laugh as Karmai's feistiness was lightweight, turning me on.

"It's not even like that love; I just been dealing with some shit feel me?" Karmai must have been feeling the same way as she told me that she wanted to see me. I told her that I wanted to see her as well so she shot me her address so I could slide through.

Before I cut out, I woke Pudge up to tell him that I would be back in a couple of hours. Half asleep still Pudge just threw up his hands, I was out of there. Karmai lived in Lakeview on Margaret Street, it was like twenty minutes away from my spot. I had to put one in the air before I went to see Karmai, my boy had some Happy runtz and some Blueberry Gelato that I was blowing on before I showed up. I didn't know if Karmai smoked so I texted her to ask her if she did.

{Hey do you smoke? I got some fire}

Karmai responded, *{Hell Yeah lol}* that's all I needed to know. I knew that we were about to fuck for real. It had been a minute since I hit some ass, so I was ready to get my fuck on, I felt bad for Karmai because I was about to go deep sea diving all up in that pussy.

My mind was right as I pulled up to Karmai's apartment, there she was looking out of her window looking like she was ready to get down. She had on what looked like a negligee that was revealing all of her goodies. My manhood was dancing in my pants with anticipation, Karmai was about to get a first-class fucking for real. The closer I got to her apartment she really started showing me what I was in for. With one hand rubbing on her breast and her other hand in between her legs, Karmai was pressed up against her window as if she was a worker in the red-light district of Amsterdam.

I was beyond turned on as I made my way through her gate towards her apartment door. She stayed upstairs in number #56, so I jogged up the stairs ready to see Karmai in person. Right, when I was about to knock on the door it flung open and there stood Karmai. She was even more beautiful in person as her purple thong sat perfectly on her pie. Having on a purple bra to match highlighted her supple breast that was finished off with her already perky nipples.

This shit was about to be major, reaching out with her left hand Karmai welcomed me inside her spot. Our savage instincts took over as we both pounced on each other with an aggressive undertone. Hands wandered everywhere as we allowed our sexual nature to take over.

"Oh yes right there don't stop" Karmai let it be known that she was enjoying my finger inside of her walls. We were barely inside of her apartment as the energy kicked up a notch. Wanting to have more room we headed into her bedroom.

Once we were inside her room Karmai turned into a different person. It was like her whole mood changed once we laid down on her bed, Pandora's box became all the way opened as Karmai put all of her skills on display. This woman had an insatiable desire, and I was more than ready to fulfill all her needs. Time stood still as we fucked and talked until I had to cut out.

"I truly enjoyed you Mr. Alzir." Karmai said as her tongue rolled across her lips. This session was exactly what I needed to reset my mind. Before I left, I told Karmai that we would definitely be seeing each other again. Her smile conveyed that she was happy to hear that, I walked over and placed a kiss on her cheek then like strike three I was out. As I walked to my car, I hit up Pudge to see what he was doing,

"What's good bruh you up? I'm about to come to swoop you so we can go get D," Pudge responded that he was ready, so I made my way to the house. When I pulled up Pudge was already outside waiting on me. He hopped in the car, and we made our way to the San Francisco airport to pick up Darhino. Traffic flowed at a pace allowing us to arrive at the airport with ten minutes to spare. Finding a spot in short-term parking we waited on D to get in. After like thirty-five minutes Darhino walked up on us ready to hear about Mayne.

"What's good? So, what happened to Mayne." D wasted no time getting to the point, you could see the pain coming in as D's eyes began to water. Mayne was our boy, he was family, so this pain hit way different for all of us. None of us were prepared to move forward without Mayne, ring, ring, I answered, and it was Kenyon.

"Bruh, we need to chill on shit right now don't you think?" Kenyon's words fell on def ears as I ignored him as if he didn't exist. I had to get my head back in the game so that we could make this right for Mayne.

"Look, as much as I know we need to chill for a minute, we also have major shit going down, Mayne would want us to get ours and you know I'm telling the truth, so let's finish what we started for Mayne".

The looks on my boy's faces said it all, we were going to get payback for Mayne, and at the same time change the entire drug game. Of course, Kenyon disagreed but I couldn't trip on that right now. The first thing I had to do was fix shit with Mykola. We couldn't afford to fuck up our plug with him for anything.

I decided to call him to attempt to squash any beef that he may be having with us. Mykola extended his condolences for Mayne before telling me that we were good. He told me that he knew that I was dealing with a heavy heart right now and that we would pick back up on our business when we were ready. Before hanging up the phone Mykola said something to me that stuck.

"You know if you get Yakiv, his father will do anything to make sure he's safe" Mykola's info was just what I needed to hear, shit was about to heat up around the city. At that moment I realized that I needed to meet up with this Yakiv character, he was the piece that could connect all the dots and I needed to know everything about what happened to Mayne.

I had Pudge reach out to Mykola to get the number for Yakiv, he reached back out to me letting me know that Yakiv was hanging in the Avenues on 47th. That was more than enough information for me, now all I needed to do was get everyone together so that we could put a play in motion.

Chapter 3
Inferno

With the murder of Mayne still fresh on our minds, we were all moving just a little slower than usual. "Hey, I wanna holla at y'all real quick," I said to Pudge and Darhino.

Kenyon was at work doing what he always does, he didn't kick it with us that much when it came to this street shit. He tried his hardest to separate the business world and the street life, but it was a thin line when it came to both. The only thing that really mattered to us was finding out what exactly happened to Mayne.

It was time to ruffle some feathers and I knew exactly where to start. I made sure that the number that Mykola gave me was authentic by calling to see who answered. Both times that I called the same male voice picked up confirming that it was indeed Yakiv's phone. I knew that he had deep security with him at all times, so chess moves would be needed in order to achieve our goal. This would be a once-in-a-lifetime opportunity for us to make this happen and I wasn't going to let anything stop that.

Ring, Ring,

"Hello, what's going on, beautiful?" Karmai's voice was a welcoming sound that definitely put a smile on my face.

"I'm going to see you later on after I handle this business," I said to Karmai. She responded that she couldn't wait to see me, and the feeling was mutual as I couldn't wait to put my hands all over her again. We hung up the phone then I proceeded to reach out to Kenyon. I wanted to see if he could get his hands on some more of these pills so I could shoot Mykola a lil extra for the misunderstanding.

"What's good, bruh you cool?" After Kenyon let it be known that he wasn't really cool, I asked him about getting more products for Mykola.

"Bruh, I can't believe that you're still trying to do this pill shit, that's the reason Mayne ain't here anymore." I could hear in Kenyon's voice that he was over the whole hustle life shit. It was not his thing at all and after losing Mayne he really didn't want to get down with us anymore.

"Look nigga, we need you on this shit, you the only one who can get us the good pills so quit tripping for real" Kenyon didn't say shit, instead he paused for a second before hollering out,

" Fuck you Alzir! I'm done my nigga." All I heard next was the dial tone. This dude was really tripping on me. I had to holla at D to let him know what Kenyon said.

After letting D know what Kenyon said he felt it best that we go up to the hospital and talk to him. Even though I felt like we were wasting our time, we decided to shoot over to Kaiser to go holla at Kenyon and squash this shit. Pudge had smoothed things over with Mykola, so it was back on and poppin.

We arrived at Kaiser ready to chop it up with Kenyon, I wasn't sure how this shit was going to go, we both could be hard-headed at times. Lucky for us Darhino was here to mediate and keep shit calm between us. Kenyon texted me telling me that he was on his way over to us.

While we waited, I talked to D about the possibilities of our next move. For a minute now I have been wanting to link up with my dude Selwyn from Hunters Point. Him and his boys have been killing the game on the under when it comes to the pill game, he had deep connections in Silicon Valley, so I knew that we needed to hook up with him.

"What's good wit y'all?" Kenyon walked up on us in the Kaiser parking lot,

"What's up bruh?" Darhino responded while I just threw up a head nod. Kenyon hopped into the car with us so that we could get some shit straight. Crowded was an understatement as the three of us talked inside of D's overpriced and super-small Tesla.

"So, what's going on bruh? You not rocking with us anymore?" Darhino came straight out and asked Kenyon,

"Naw, it's not like that D, I didn't sign up for all the street shit though, I was cool just hooking y'all up with the pills, but this nigga At It, talking like we on some mafia type shit." I couldn't believe this nigga was really whining like a baby and shit,

"Kenyon, you knew what it was from the jump, now you're acting brand new cause we gotta get physical with this shit, what the fuck, bruh." I was pissed, this nigga getting at us like he is not crew now, over a little bump in the road. Before things went all the way left.

Darhino told us both that we needed to squash this shit cause at the end of the day we were still family. Neither one of us really didn't want to hear that but it was the truth, we have been boyz way too long for something like this to come in between us. We pounded it out and shit was back on like we never left it.

Now that things were back on track it was time to make things right with Mykola. Kenyon was able to get some extra Oxycodone for us to include with what we were giving Mykola, I knew this would put us back on top with him, especially after having him waiting for a minute.

I hit him up to let him know that shit was all good, Mykola was juiced and ready to get the deal done. This time we were having him come to us instead of meeting somewhere, we didn't want any surprises or distractions this go round. The meet was set, 8:00 pm was the time that we agreed upon to get the deal done. It was going to be one of those deals where both sides will be able to eat from this for a very long time.

Although Mykola had plans to keep some of the pills for himself, he was still a businessman at the end of the day, with the remaining pills he had he was planning on turning Silicon Valley all the way out. His connections out that way were in the habit of paying at least five to ten more dollars for that good shit. That was nothing to the many millionaires that lived out that way.

Silicon Valley was the new hot spot for the upper epsilon, the who's who of the tech world all lived out that way and you could always find someone looking for that new hype. This was perfect for us in order to expand our business into other areas of the Bay. We had the city on lock already having the majority of the city sold up with our products. San Francisco loved us and now we wanted the Valley to get hooked as well.

The remainder of our time was spent reaching out to some of the players out in Silicon Valley, we knew that we had to watch our moves out that way especially since the Melnyk family had the bulk of the pill game on lock out there. That didn't stop us though, we knew that there were still plenty of areas that were just waiting to be put on to that new, new and we were going to be the ones to bring it to them.

They say, never burn a bridge because you never know when you may have to cross back over it. This was the case with Olou Musa, he was a Nigerian boss who ran pretty much all of the dope that came through the Bay Area. His family settled in the upper Haight Street area of the city, big, huge houses with private surroundings made up this exclusive neighborhood.

Musa wasn't the caring type; his family really was known for putting motherfuckers into the ground. You couldn't move any drugs in the city if you weren't going through the Musa family. I've been solid with the family for some time now, we had some dealings back in the day and have been fucking with each other ever since. As long as you were a man of your word you would never have any issues with Olou, but if you don't keep your word with him, you will probably find body parts spread throughout the city.

Olou only understood one thing and that was money, as long as you had that dollar amount right, he didn't care who you were. Knowing that I would need some extra soldiers to go up against the Melnyk family, I reached out to Olou to see if he could send me some hittas to go to war with.

"What's good wit my boy?" I asked Olou who was on the other end of the phone coughing up his lungs.

"Excuse me, bro I'm blowing on that fire," Olou said as the final few coughs came through the phone.

"It's been a minute since I heard from you what's going on?" I began telling Olou about my issue with the Melnyk family, as he listened to my story, I could tell that he wasn't going to want to lend me any soldiers for this battle. His interruptions, while I was talking to him, let me know that he wasn't with it.

"Real talk bro I don't have any issues with the Melnyk family, so I don't want to create any you feel me?" I couldn't believe that this dude was on the other end of this phone sounding like a straight bitch.

"So, you can't do me this solid bruh? I thought we were better than that for real." Olou began running drag to me,

"Now come on man, you know we are solid bro." This nigga must have thought that I was some clown ass dude, usually, I would be concerned about burning a bridge but in this case, I was like fuck Olou if he couldn't do this for me.

"So, are you in or what bruh?" I waited for an answer from Olou.

"I'm going to have to pass on this one bro."

Not wanting to create an issue at this moment I just responded, "Ok." I think Olou knew that I was disappointed in him", he said before he hung up.

"My bad bro but if you need anything else I got you."

I just hung up the phone and started thinking of a new play for us to make. Since I was unable to get the soldiers that I needed, I decided to stick with our original plan to grab up Yakiv.

Now with a solid plan in motion, it was time to relieve some long overdue stress. Wanting to get into some freaky shit I called up Karmai, after four rings I hung up the phone. No answer let me know that she was out and about enjoying herself.

Not having lots of time before we met up with Mykola, I shot over to Cookies on Haight to grab up some more trees. My boy Berner had some new strands in, and I wanted to cop me a few. The Haight was poppin as the tourists walked block after block peeping all the sites.

Now that I had my goods, I made my way back to the house to get ready for the meeting with Mykola. Less than an hour before the meeting, me, Pudge and Darhino, discussed the possibilities of working with Selwyn after we wrapped up this deal with Mykola.

"My only thing with working with ole boy is, they say he can't be trusted." D didn't like the thought of us moving with Selwyn and his crew, he felt it would bring too much attention to what we were doing.

The Hunters were Selwyn's crew, and they were the dirty type, they would harm kids and old people alike, and they had no code or respect for nothing at all. They had turned Hunters Point into a battlefield of survival, those who could stay did, and those who couldn't move onto other parts of the Bay area.

This move may have not been in our long-term plan, but for now, teaming up with Selwyn and his boyz would definitely give us the manpower that we needed to go at the Melnyk family head-on. The sound of the doorbell let me know that Mykola was here, my hands started to itch as I knew the money had arrived. Pudge made his way over to open the door,

"Welcome bruh, what's going on?" Mykola entered with two of his men with him.

"Hey, my man Pudge what's going on brother?" Mykola and Pudge greeted each other with a firm handshake, afterwards Mykola introduced the two gentlemen that were with him.

"My brothers, these two here with me are my right and left-hand men, Yuri and Lim, they are solid folks." after the awkwardness of greeting each other was out of the way, we got down to the business at hand.

"So let me see what you have for me, Pudge?" Mykola said with an anxious voice, right at that moment Darhino walked over with a duffle bag full of pills. D placed the bag right in front of Mykola so that he could see directly inside, as his hands reappeared from inside of the bag, they were filled with smaller bags filled with pills of all types.

"You motherfuckers are about to make a killing with this shit." Mykola was juiced as Yuri and Lim also became wide-eyed at the possibilities of what these pills would bring. Starting to talk to each other in Ukrainian, Yuri and Lim set off red flags with D.

"What are you motherfuckers saying? Speak English when you're around us" you could feel the energy in the room change as now all eyes were on Darhino.

"Hey everyone calm down, there is no need to let things get out of hand," Mykola uttered but like pit bulls ready to attack, it was a straight fuck you stare down between D, Yuri, and Lim. This shit had to chill the fuck out real fast, it was too much money on the table to be tripping off of little shit.

"VD, come on bruh, we got our bread, let's cut" Darhino smirked before stopping his mean mug towards Yuri and Lim. Pudge had been counting the money making sure that every dollar was accounted for".

"We good, At It." With confirmation in hand, we politely escorted Mykola, Yuri, and Lim out of the spot. Once they were gone, we celebrated our victory. Pudge poured us some shots to kick the festivities off. I wanted to throw a stack in the air, so I grabbed a handful of money and tossed it up to the sky. It was dope watching the money fall back down to the floor and thinking we are just getting started with this pill shit. Next on our to-do list was taking care of this Yakiv dude, for now, though it was turn-uptime and we all needed to release some stress.

Chapter 4
Chaos

We decided to go to Larry Flynt's Hustlers Club on Kearny Street. They weren't known for having the thickest chicks, but they definitely had some eye candy for us to look at. I was about to blow several stacks up in the place, I was definitely about to change someone's night this evening.

"Nigga you already know I'm about to hit some ass up in here," Pudge said causing us to break out laughing at him. It had been a minute since we kicked it with Kenyon, so I hit him up to see if he wanted to come to kick it with us.

"What's up, my dude? We at Larry Flynt's slide through." Kenyon sounded half asleep, once he was able to get a clear mind, he told me that he would come through.

Back to the bitches it was, I had three rubber bands equaling three stacks each, I began throwing it up in the air watching it fall back down like rain. A few dancers made their way over to where me and the boyz were chilling, it was about to go down in our section. With asses flapping in the wind and breast glistening, our area was now the place to be at.

Pudge wasted no time finding him a dancer to take back to the private room, we knew what he was back there doing so we just let him get his smash on. Darhino, also had a little dancer who was all over him like she wanted to fuck, it must have been something in the air because not even ten minutes later and D was gone as well. I stayed in our section waiting on Kenyon to get here. Damn near an hour later, Kenyon came through looking all refreshed and shit.

"It's about time nigga what took so long?" I said to a smiling Kenyon.

"You know I had to get fresh bruh, I was asleep when you called me," Kenyon replied before heading to the bar for a drink. Now that he was here, I headed over to the private room to see if Pudge and D were still back there. As soon as I walked into the room all I could hear was the sounds of fucking, so I knew that they both were still back here. I cut out and met up with Kenyon at the bar, when I walked up on him, he was talking to this badass-looking Asian chick. The baby looked like she had some black in her family as her ass poked out like *"HELLO"* I had to do a double take. She was hella thick. Kenyon was nursing his drink, but baby girl was throwing hers down like she was on drink champs and shit.

"What's your name love?" Kenyon asked,

"Prima, but you can call me Lai," she replied with her sexy ass. Ordering more shots had us talking up a storm, Lai let it be known that she was mixed with black and Asian, I knew that though, you could tell by looking at her. Kenyon was blitzed, it didn't take much for him to get lit, finally, both Pudge and Darhino came walking over to the bar.

"What's upper with my guys?" Pudge was juiced, you could tell that this nigga just fucked because he was cheesing like a big ass kid. Darhino also had that pleased look on his face.

"Both of y'all look like you ain't never had no pussy before" laughs erupted as we all were feeling pretty damn good. With the night slowly coming to an end, we were ready to call it a night. 2:37 am.

Right, when we decided to go, in walked the after-club crew. These were a group of dudes who live for the club life, you know, being seen by the same broads, doing the same shit every weekend, yeah them bitch ass dudes with no real life.

They must have been feeling hard this early morning because like money being thrown all over the ground, chaos showed up causing us to knock out these bitch ass club dudes. All you could see was hands being thrown, and bodies hitting the floor at a rapid pace.

Darhino was knocking fools the fuck out, one by one they all went down like bowling pins. With a few cuts and scratches on us, we made our way up out of Larry Flynt's. Outside, we all looked at each other and started laughing as if it was a comedy show.

"This has been one hell of a day don't y'all agree?" Pudge asked us, and we all responded saying, "Hell yeah." With little time left before the sun would be coming up, we made our way to the house.

Sleep was becoming something that was getting harder to get, my body was telling me that I needed to shut it all the way down for a second to reboot. Having no choice but to listen, as soon as we made it home, I hit my bed and traveled off into dreamland. Making sure that I wouldn't be interrupted I placed my phone on silent mode, I truly needed some rest, and I didn't want anything to stop that from happening.

Kenyon wound up staying over with us as well due to him being fucked up from the drink. He was the only one of us who had his own spot right now, it was by choice that Pudge and D stayed together. We liked having big ass parties and shit, plus us living together allowed us to have this big house that we had.

We stayed on Masonic in a Duplex; our spot was considered the buss down because we stayed with some type of event going on over here. The ladies love coming over to the spot and relaxing in the sauna, shit gets wild up in here for real. If the walls could talk it would probably be a New York Times bestseller over here.

We have had some crazy nights leading to even crazier mornings, it's something about being in an exclusive neighborhood that makes you feel free and uninhibited. Plus, we kept the fire trees, so people loved coming over to blow with us, that usually led to some kind of sexual episode involving multiple women. We have been trying to get Kenyon to move in with us, but he's still not with it. For now, it's party central at the spot and we love it.

The morning arrived and it was a new day, the focus today was getting more info on Yakiv Melnyk, he was still the piece to the puzzle for us to be able to find out what happened to Mayne. I also wanted to holla at Selwyn about making a move on the Melnyk family at one of their establishments. I knew that they had a few restaurants throughout the Bay Area, so I figured that would be a good place to catch them slipping.

I put D onto getting more info about the daily operations and how they work. Pudge was going to reach out to his Ukrainian connections to see what he could come up with. It was go time, and we didn't want to fall behind on taking out the ops. Kenyon must have known that he was on my mind as my phone started ringing,

"What's good bruh? Where are you at?" Kenyon asked, sounding excited. I told him that I was still at the house about to get my day started. He let me know that he had some more pills for me, he also let me know that he had a plug at the hospital who was looking for that white girl. That was music to my ears because I didn't want to be sitting on this product too long, now that we were getting that yola from Selwyn shit was poppin in a major way.

We were getting money left and right and it didn't seem that it was going to slow down anytime soon. The saying, if it's too good it probably is, was starting to manifest right in front of my eyes. Right when I thought that we were on the path to victory, greed showed its ugly face in the form of a money-hungry Selwyn. I thought that we had an understanding, but now this dude wants to renegotiate our deal because he sees all the money that we're getting with this pill shit.

He wasn't even into the whole pill game until I talked to him about it, this nigga was a coke and heroin dealer, he never wanted to deal with pills until now. I learned a long time ago that greed will get you killed, it's always that one dude who always has to have more than everyone else, that's the dude that I would never do business with because that type of person always wants more than they deserve.

Selwyn wanted to meet at the Dope Era store on Broadway to chop it up with me about some pills. What he did not know was, I wasn't giving him the plug on the pills, so he was going to have to get them from someone else. I arrived at Dope Era, Mista Fab and the Unkster were outside politicking with the people. Fab was a figure in the community and he was always doing something for the city of Oakland.

We walked down the street to discuss the pill situation, it was something about Selwyn's energy that didn't feel right to me. Usually, he is upbeat and talkative, but he was the total opposite of that today. We were damn near at the corner where Cookies is located before Selwyn asked me why I wasn't fucking with him on the pills. Kind of catching me off guard I responded by saying, "I don't think it's a good idea for you to jump into that lane." The way his eyebrow raised from my statement instantly let me know that it was about to be a problem.

"What do you mean by that? Selwyn asked with an aggressive tone. Not wanting to escalate the situation I replied telling him that it's a different game and that it's nothing like the coke game as far as the clientele is concerned. With a confused look on his face, Selwyn's next statement let me know that he may become a problem that I don't need.

"How are you going to tell me that it is not my lane? Do you know who I am?" After Selwyn's comment no longer did, I think we had a problem, I knew for a fact that we did. I didn't want to cause a scene, so I started walking back towards my car which was double parked on Broadway.

"*WHERE THE FUCK YOU THINK YOU GOING BRUH?*" My radar shot up like a hunting dog once it's locked in on its prey, that feeling of adrenaline ignited me getting me into savage mode.

"*I KNOW YOU HEAR ME BRUH DON'T MAKE ME GET LOUDER.*" Now I was beyond pissed off, with my pole snug in the small of my back and my game face on, I stopped and turned around to address this bitch ass nigga.

"You got something to say to me bruh?" An elderly Chinese man slowly walked across the intersection. A white couple walked down the stairs towards the BART station, and an OG walked out of the Cookies store. I pulled out and two-piece Selwyn right where he stood.

Screams rang out from the few people who were on the block caught up in the crossfire. I took off running towards my car before anyone could really grasp what had happened, as I sped off, I couldn't help but holler out because I knew that I had fucked up.

"FUCK, FUCK, FUCK." Slamming my driver's hand on the dashboard only made things worse for me. My frustration was kicking my ass and my decision-making was way off. I had to get off the streets before anyone started looking for me.

I hit Kenyon to see if I could kick it at his spot for a minute. Without asking me any questions Kenyon told me of course I could come to kick it with him. On my way over to his spot, I called Pudge and Darhino to tell them what happened. D let me know that they would meet me over at Kenyon's spot.

Still pumped up off of the adrenaline I attempted to smoke some trees to try and relax my nerves. The weed smoke helped but not enough to erase the fact that I just laid Selwyn down in broad daylight. I didn't know what to do at the moment other than ask God for forgiveness.

My thoughts were spiraling into that place you don't come back from. It wasn't about me killing Selwyn, it was the way I chose to do it that was going to bring me unwanted bullshit. I wanted to keep this side of the game out of reach for as long as I could, my temper did not allow that to manifest and now I was going to have to deal with the Hunters once they got wind of this. I just wanted to make some real money, instead, I'm right back in the belly of the beast just trying to survive another day. Kenyon lived on Broderick Street in these fly-ass apartments, they were overpriced but the area was worth the money. As soon as Kenyon saw me, he knew that something was wrong.

"What happened bruh?" I couldn't even put my words together to begin to explain to Kenyon the amount of shit I was in. All I could do was shake my head as Kenyon asked me again what happened. My words sounded as if they were moving in slow motion as I replayed what happened for Kenyon, he just looked at me as if he didn't know me, his look cut me deep because I knew I had really fucked up.

"Damn, bruh what the fuck, man I don't know what to say Alzir."

This wasn't a place that I wanted to be in, but it was definitely the place I was at. It was all or nothing now, the gloves were off, and I was prepared to fight for my life. Pudge and Darhino arrived at the spot right at that moment, right when they walked inside, I started telling them what happened. Their faces displayed looks of concern as I continued to tell them what went down. By the end of the story, Pudge was just shaking his head, Darhino had a lost look on his face and that tripped me out because I have never seen him worried about anything.

"I don't know what to say bruh, you really just put us in the fire though," Darhino said, barely looking in my direction. All I could do was apologize to my guys for putting them in this position,

"I'm truly sorry y'all, I know I fucked up." My apology, although sincere, wasn't going to change how the fellas felt right now. I had to give them some time to process all of this shit, I had to process this as well knowing that Selwyn had hittas who were relentless when it came to riding for him.

This was draining me to the point of no return, for now, I let my mind rest hoping that when I wake back up I have more of a plan to go with. If not, things are going to go from zero to a hundred real fast. The dreams started to take me away the deeper my thoughts rested. This was the only time that I felt at complete peace, no other time of the day did I feel peace like the peace I feel when I'm sleeping. Unbothered and worry-free is the only way that I can explain the feeling of getting good rest gives me. As my eyes started flickering trying to stay open, I could feel my body crashing.

Buzz, Buzz, Buzz. I looked at the phone and suddenly I was up. The number was one that I was familiar with, especially since I had recently called it. Yakiv Melnyk's name came across my screen and just like that the game was on. I answered wanting to see what he wanted.

"Hello this is Alzir, what's going on?" Silence came from the other end of the phone,

"Hello, I know it's you Yakiv so why don't you tell me what kind of business you were doing with Mayne" *(a whisper)*

"Remember, even in a group of angels you will always find a demon."

Chapter 5
Secrets

Staring into my phone I didn't know what to do. I was totally lost on what the fuck was going on. I started really trying to figure out what kind of shit Mayne was involved in. I knew that whatever it was. This was the second time now that someone made that statement; it had to be something worth him losing his life over.

A part of me wanted to call Yakiv back but I couldn't bring myself to do so. Nothing registered for me though as my mind drew blanks trying to figure out what that statement meant. Unable to fall asleep I stayed up thinking about what Mayne could have been doing with Yakiv. Nothing came to me as I pondered over what the meaning could be behind this statement.

I wasn't getting anywhere with this shit; I was only making myself more stressed about it. Finally, time started getting the best of me, and my eyes were able to stay closed now allowing me to get some sleep. Just when I was able to feel my body starting to decompress the sun was once again greeting me as if it was our first-time meeting.

The yawns flowed as I laid down on the top of my bed in an effort to grab up anything else, I could get. I was so tired, but I knew I had to get up and strike at Yakiv before he struck me first. All this shit because I no longer wanted to depend on anyone. Who would have known that all this extra came with wanting to make money? I haven't even gotten back with Karmai due to the fact that I was out here hustling. I had to slow down and get my life in order, the only thing was, I didn't have your typical lifestyle so what is the norm to everyone else, maybe something that is foreign to me. Whatever it is I had to figure it out sooner than later.

"HEY, COME IN HERE," Darhino called out from the living room. Me and Pudge walked in at the same time looking to see why D was hollering. Kenyon showed up shortly after still looking like he was drunk,

"Why are you yelling bruh?" Kenyon asked with a groggy voice.

"You need to get out of town bruh, the Hunters know that you killed Selwyn and they're coming for you." Not really knowing what I wanted to say, I told D I would go somewhere for a minute. Pudge and Kenyon were stuck, unable to believe how shit was turning out. I grabbed up as much bread as I had in the house along with a few bags of clothes.

We had a spot out in Reno where we stayed when we needed to get out of the city. This was going to be home for me until shit died down. I knew that the Hunters wouldn't rest until they had my heart in their hands. I truly regretted getting my guys involved in my bullshit, my fucking temper has always been my downfall in life.

If I would have just smacked Selwyn around shit would be different, yeah, I would have an issue with the Hunters, but it wouldn't be on this level. Unfortunately, that isn't my reality, instead, I had to rock this motherfucker's whole world, that's just how I get down at the end of the day. With my bags in hand, I was off to Reno to escape the madness for a split second. There was a part of me that felt like I was running away, but then I remember D saying to me, "This shit will be temporary bruh trust me, just let things die down then you can come back, feel me?"

If it would have been anyone other than D I wouldn't have gone to Reno. I knew that he was only looking out for my safety, but I was concerned for his safety and the safety of my guys just as much.

One month later...

"What's good At It? Are you ready to come back home?"

I have been waiting a month to hear those words. I told Darhino "Hell yeah." Then, I was out of Reno heading back to the life I know and loved.

During the time I was gone, the Hunters took a few losses as their organization started to become frazzled within. The team held down the hustle while I was on hiatus keeping shit going with Mykola, as well as a new player on the board.

Connor Klein was this super smart rich dude out of Seattle, he moved down to the Bay Area a few years back and has been silently changing the game on the under. Recently Connor moved from Menlo Park to the city and is currently living in the Nob Hill area of Frisco.

He heard that we were the ones to be in business with, so it only made sense that we hooked up. Like most greedy motherfuckers Connor wanted to get into the coke game but didn't want to get his hands dirty. Instead, he thought that since we were niggas, we should be the ones taking all the street risk.

What he didn't know was that he was also going to be paying a higher tax on the dope since we were the ones taking all the risk. Agreeing to our terms came easy as Connor anxiously broke us off our cut. The road of opportunity was getting wider by the minute, and we were riding hard as fuck on it. The devil has a way of letting you know that he is close, it never fails. With all this good news going on for us, it only made sense that we get some bad news along with it.

Buzz, Buzz.

"Hello this is Alzir, talk to me." At first, I thought that someone was playing on the phone due to the silence, but then my attention was caught once Yakiv Melnyk started to talk.

"I know you think that I had something to do with Mayne being murdered but I didn't, you should be looking closer at those around you."

Yakiv was gone and once again my mind was left to wonder what the fuck was going on.

"If it wasn't Yakiv who had Mayne killed then who was it?" I said to myself as the unknown was taking me on an uncertain journey. I needed to holla at the team to let them know what was said by Yakiv. I reached out and told everyone to meet me at the spot asap, with the exception of Kenyon who was at work getting his bread.

When I arrived at the spot Pudge was there waiting, D wasn't here yet, so we waited on him to arrive. Twenty minutes later D walked through the door with a concerned look on his face.

"So, what is really going on bruh?" Darhino asked, wanting to get to the bottom of this shit. I started telling both of them what was said to me by Yakiv. The more I talked the more their facial expressions changed. Pudge was starting to look angrier the more I repeated what was said to me. After I was done telling them what Yakiv said, D still looked puzzled.

"So bruh even if it wasn't Yakiv who killed Mayne, then who was it, and what does that statement about the angels have to do with anything?"

Now my face was puzzled after hearing D. He had me thinking about all this shit on a much bigger scale. Yakiv wasn't telling me everything and I needed him to, so I decided to reach out to him to see if he would meet me somewhere to talk in person. Although he didn't feel that it was a good idea to meet in person, Yakiv agreed to meet me at Bookah's Gourmet Pot Pies in Emeryville.

I let D and Pudge know that I was meeting up with Yakiv. Before I left, I grabbed my pole just in case. On my way over to the restaurant, I kept thinking about that statement, for the life of me I couldn't figure it out. Hopefully, this conversation with Yakiv brings me the closure that I know we all need.

I pulled up to Bookah's around 7:26 pm, I wasn't sure if Yakiv was here or not yet, so I made my way inside to see if he was there. Guessing that I beat him here, I grabbed us a table and ordered some fried plantains while I waited for Yakiv to arrive. Fifteen minutes later Yakiv arrived but he wasn't alone.

I instantly thought that he was here on some setup-type shit, so my jaws began to clinch from anger and anticipation. As I watched out from the restaurant window, I noticed that only Yakiv was getting out of the car to come inside. This made me relax a little knowing that he wasn't here for any extra drama. Yakiv walked into the restaurant and made his way towards the table I was sitting at.

"Alzir, I take it." After confirming that we are both who we said we are, we began talking about Mayne. Yakiv started off by saying that he gives his deepest condolences for my loss. Next, he began telling me a story that had me feeling as if I never knew who Mayne really was. The more he talked the more the pain kicked in.

All this time I had been thinking that Mayne was my brother, when in actuality according to Yakiv, Mayne had plans to cut us all the way out of the loop. Yakiv continued saying that Mayne was only loyal to money, he told me that Mayne had got real close to his father and that Anton Melnyk himself was taking a liking to Mayne.

Everything was good until Mayne showed Anton who his real loyalty was with. Yakiv said that Anton asked Mayne to take care of something for him, he went on to say that his father didn't think that he would agree to do it, but once he did agree that's when he knew that Mayne couldn't be trusted because he would go against his own for the money.

I couldn't believe what Yakiv was saying to me, but the cold thing about it was I believed him. Mayne was out here cutting deals with whoever would cash him out, this whole time I thought that he was family when in actuality he was just a money-hungry ass nigga who got himself killed because he had no loyalty to shit. The next thing that came out of Yakiv's mouth put me in a weird position,

"Even though it was my father who had Mayne killed, I didn't have anything to do with that, and neither did any of my men. It was all my father's call. I understand you have to do what you have to do, I just wanted you to know the truth."

I sat there in disbelief; this dude just told me some unreal shit and I was really trying to wrap my mind around it. Yakiv stood up and was getting ready to make his way out of the restaurant,

"Hey, one last thing. What the fuck does that statement have to do with us?"

Yakiv looked back at me and said, "You guys were the angels to Mayne always having his back, but Mayne was the demon who no matter what always got in his own way. My father would ask him all the time how he could be so unloyal to you guys when you guys were always there for him."

As Yakiv walked out of the restaurant, I sat in my chair unable to move. I thought about what else Mayne said about us to Anton Melnyk. My mind was torturing me because I no longer knew what was real, and what was fake.

Chapter 6
Vengeance

I must have sat in my chair for thirty minutes before I finally got up to leave. Yakiv had just come clean on what happened between his family and Mayne. I knew that he was in an awkward position by telling me this. I also respected him for telling me.

I couldn't wait to get home so that I could tell Pudge and Darhino what was really going on. I just hoped that they were ready to receive this information about Mayne. Telling Kenyon wasn't even on my radar right now, I knew that he couldn't take hearing the news about Mayne. They were boyz as we all were.

"Ring, Ring."

I started not to answer once I saw that it was Mykola, I had to see what he wanted. "What's good Mykola?"

He replied that he needed some more work asap and that he wanted to increase his amount. All this was sounding good to me but right now my head wasn't in the game, and I didn't want to play. Nevertheless, I told Mykola that I would get him straight in a few hours. He was content with that so I reassured him that he would get a visit from me later on this evening.

When I pulled up at home a part of me just wanted to say fuck it all, this was becoming way more than I ever wanted it to become and it was taking a toll on me for real. When I walked inside the house both Pudge and D were sitting in the living room. They both had looks on their faces that were saying, what the fuck. I sat down on the small couch and began telling them what was said to me. Once I finished talking no words were said, only looks of confusion showed up on both the faces of Pudge and D.

"Say, something man," I said trying to get a response from one of them. It was def silent as we just sat there not knowing what to say. After like three minutes of silence Pudge finally said something, "I don't know what to say bruh, if this shit is true that nigga never was the crew at all." Pudge was pissed the fuck off, as was Darhino.

"Naw bruh, I can't believe that shit, not Mayne, he wouldn't do us like that." Darhino was having a hard time accepting that Mayne may have been the ops in real life.

"Fuck that, fuck that, call this Yakiv dude back. I want to hear this shit for myself."

D was becoming upset the more he thought about it. I called Yakiv and, like watching a rerun, I listened again as he told Darhino and Pudge the exact same story that he just finished telling me. Now to see the looks on their faces hit differently as they both now knew the ugly truth about Mayne.

"The fact that dude's own father saw how disloyal this nigga was, really don't sit well with me bruh," Pudge said angrily,

"So even though we were like angels to this nigga, he still chose to be a demon towards us, I'm fucking hot bruh."

Pudge was fuming after thinking about everything that was said today. With all that said we still had an issue that needed to be resolved, regardless of what went down Mayne was our folks at one point. To know that Anton Melnyk took it upon himself to kill Mayne didn't sit well with us.

We were at a crossroads, and we had to make a decision on what we were going to do. Before we made a final decision on anything we hit up Kenyon to put him in the loop. Just like I thought Kenyon was taking the news extremely hard, for him, it wasn't about the disloyalty that Mayne showed, for Kenyon it was the fact that we all had grown up together and before shit went left, we were family.

Kenyon hung up the phone and that was the end of our conversation with him. The remainder of the evening went by fast as none of us could think straight. I knew that I was supposed to be meeting Mykola later on, but I really wasn't feeling it. I didn't want to

BAY BIZZNESS   111

fake on him, so I asked a friend of mine named Prell to drop the shit off for me.

Prell was my potna from around the way, he lived in Fillmoe and has always been a real solid dude. He wasn't in the life but from time to time he handled some errands for me. In return I put a few dollars in his pocket to show my appreciation. I called up Mykola to let him know that Prell would be meeting him at Ella Hill Hutch gym to drop off the work. Mykola didn't care who brought him the work as long as he got it.

Now that I had that covered, I decided to go off the grid for a while. Shit has been hectic as fuck, and I needed a break from the madness. Knowing that it has been a minute, I hit up Karmai. She was pleasantly surprised to hear from me, I was happy to hear from her as well. My body needed to be around some nectar and Karmai had that sweet juice that I craved.

She told me that she couldn't wait to see me before hanging up the phone. I took a nice hot shower to get the day's frustrations off of me, I was ready now to put in work, I rolled up a few blunts then headed over to Karmai's house.

The rest of the crew were at the house lounging, staying out of the way, we all knew that shit was going to get crazy before it ever got right. So, for now I chose to take all of my frustrations out on Karmai's beautiful body. She hit my line to tell me that she was leaving the front door open for me to come straight inside. I knew that her body was in need as well, so I most definitely came to please.

Not bragging, but a nigga beat it down. It was on from the time I walked in the door. Every inch of Karmai's body I managed to devour. She was busting off as if she was part machine or something.

Our bodies sweaty and hot set the tone for what was one of my most exhilarating sessions to date. We were connected physically in a way that made it beyond easy to have a strong mental connection as well. Karmai wasn't the overbearing type, she allowed me to come and go as I pleased.

Even though she wasn't tripping off of our situation like it was a relationship, I gave Karmai the utmost respect when it came to her knowing who I really am. I didn't play any head games with her, and she respected that about me. With or without a title Karmai, was the only woman that I felt I could talk to about my life and what it is to be me. She didn't come with judgement or the typical lame female movements, instead Karmai manifested confidence throughout her whole aura.

After another mini session Karmai dove off into a deep sleep, before leaving I rubbed her down with some cocoa butter that had her smelling like delicious treats. I threw my clothes on and headed back to my spot, this energy was definitely what I needed to push through and prepare me for whatever may come my way. When I got back to the house Kenyon was there, he was talking to Pudge about this plug he met through the hospital, and he wanted to turn her on to us. Glad that I had stumbled in on that conversation when I did, Pudge must have forgotten that we have just gone into a new move with Conner.

"Not to be all in the business but Pudge you do remember that we're fucking with Conner for a minute, right?" I could tell that Pudge had forgotten about Conner by the look on his face.

"My bad bruh, I did forget about the ole boy," Pudge said, as his memory kicked back into focus. Before I completely shut Kenyon's idea down, I wanted to hear more about it.

"Tell me about this chic Kenyon, what's her deal?" Kenyon started telling me how Linda Kurtz, this physical therapist up at his job, wanted to come up on coke. Based on what Kenyon was saying she wanted to spend big bread on some yola.

He went on to say that she was planning on having a big get-together and that some of her guests were into that white girl real heavy. Her money was peanuts in comparison to what we were about to be making off of Conner. Still, I could see that Kenyon wanted me to hook this up, so I did it for him this one time.

I let Kenyon know that he was responsible for getting the money from ole girl, he told me that it was all good, so I hooked him up with some product for Linda. Having that lightweight business out of the way allowed me to focus on this move with Conner. He knew some folks who wanted that real weight, from pills to yola.

His people were looking to spend top dollar for that top-tier product. Conner himself wanted to cop some pills for this high-power lunch that he was throwing for one of his politician friends. I wanted to kill two birds with one stone, so I told Conner to bring his friends to Hawthorn club around 9:00 pm.

All our ducks were in a row, the big payday was right around the corner. It had been a minute since I hollered at Olou, I just wanted to tap in with him and check his temperature.

"What's good with my guy?" I said to Olou,

"Aww shit, it's the gangsta himself, what's good wit you playa?"

Olou always had jokes when he wasn't running motherfuckers into the dirt. I told him that I was just tapping in with him, I knew that it was a reason why I hit up Olou today. He told me that word was, Anton Melnyk was starting to feel his pockets getting a little light now that we were in the game fully. He also made the comment to some folks that we know in common, that we were no longer the angels that he thought we were.

As soon as Olou revealed to me what he heard, I no longer gave a fuck about being politically correct. Moving forward, if you weren't with me, you are against me and you have to be dealt with. It was fuck it season and I was ready to get it started.

Chapter 7
The Bizzness

In this part of my life, I was calling the Sucka Free. Meaning that I wasn't caring who you were, if you were in the way you had to get rolled over. We all felt this way, Pudge, Darhino, and even Kenyon was fed up with feeling like Anton Melnyk was in the way of our climb to the top.

I reached out to Mykola to pick his brain on Anton. Like Mykola's father, Anton was a highly respected figure in this world that we played in. He was considered old school when it came to his tactics, most people wouldn't even think to go at him, but we aren't most people. We were going to go right at his neck to make sure we cut off his head.

All night we stayed up coming up with an elaborate plan to get rid of, not only Anton Melnyk but all those who posed a threat to what we were doing. This included Olou Musa, who thought that he was fooling us, but for months now we were aware that he fucked with Anton in a major way. This info came to us courtesy of one of Mykola's plugs who was a top dog in the Kushnir family. It pays to have eyes and ears all over, this way you don't miss out on anything. Wanting to get Conner right we headed over to Hawthorne club to handle the business.

We arrived about ten minutes late, but Conner wasn't tripping off of that. Hawthorne was packed and the ladies were definitely on full display. In and out like a robbery, we took care of Conner then disappeared like a magic act. We had other things to deal with that were consuming all of our time. We were about to pull off the biggest *Fuck You!* that has ever been pulled off. Still sticking to the script, we were on our grind getting all the bread that we could get out of this game.

Knowing that we were about to eliminate Anton, Olou, and the rest of their crews gave us a rush that only you get from being in a fast life. We had reached out to Anton to let him know that we were bowing out of the pill game for good, we also let Olou know that we were taking our products and heading South to start over.

Once the seeds were planted, we just sat back and waited for our time to strike. These motherfuckers must have forgotten who they were dealing with. There was no way that we were giving up all this money because one old fuck was feeling some type of way. As far as Olou was concerned he was just a casualty of the game itself, plus he had bitch ass tendencies, so he had to go.

Having both of them thinking that we were throwing a leaving-the-game celebration, we set the day for this upcoming Saturday to be our going-out party. What they didn't know was, this was going to be their going home party instead. Once we had all of them in the building, we were planning on releasing a fury of pain that would leave only us left standing in the end.

Mykola let us know that Anton was telling people that we were leaving the game because we didn't want any smoke from him. Little did he know that we were preparing to bring him all the smoke and then some. The guest list at Hawthorn's was kept to an exclusive few for this homegoing. Outside of us, we were only inviting the Musa and Melnyk family members, of course, they weren't aware that they were our special guests, but sooner than later they would know everything.

The evening couldn't have been any better as far as the weather was concerned. The stars were out, and San Francisco was shining, you could feel that something was in the air the closer it got to party time. We were already in attendance just awaiting the arrival of our special guest. One by one both families started to arrive, and you could feel death creeping into the air. After everyone was inside, we started our presentation,

"Hello, can I get everyone's attention?" I hollered out letting everyone know that it was game time. A circle formed with both families awaiting the news that we had for them, as soon as the room was somewhat quiet, I stepped into the front of the circle that was formed by both of the families.

"I know that you all are here because you think that we're leaving the game, but that's not true at all." Rumbles of conversation started flowing throughout the circle formed by the families.

"So, what exactly are you saying Alzir?" Olou asked. I paused for a second before hollering out "YEE." Knowing that both families were in here naked due to us checking weapons at the door, me, Pudge, Kenyon, and Darhno pulled out our poles and started laying everyone down with a furious barrage of shots. All you could see was the smoke filling up in the area we were in. Once the smoke cleared and the last pop from the guns went off, there were no bodies moving on the ground.

I looked over to see where Anton Melnyk was. Once I saw that he was no longer breathing I looked over at him and told him., "See motherfucker, I wanted all the smoke."

After checking to make sure that no one was alive, we all just looked at each other with the same look on our faces and said, *"IT'S THE MOTHERFUCKING BUSINESS, AND TAKING CARE OF BUSINESS IS WHAT WE DO!"*

The End.

Trust No Bitch

By Caleigh Blue

The Introduction

Vallejo, California.... Also known as the Valley Jo. The itty-bitty city by the water where it goes down. Home of the Romper Room Gang, E-40 and the Click from the Hillside, and Mac Dre from the Country Club Crest. Where cousin and buddy were combined, birthing the word cuddy, and home of the drink Cuddy Bang. The Bay Area A.K.A

The Yay Area is known for being its own world, separated from the rest of Cali, and having its own slang dictionary found on the internet.

Vallejo, California .... Where it gets grimy, street codes are broken, and every nigga is out for himself. The city where muthafuckas stay set tripping. Shit's always flying through the air like we're in the ghetto. A place where you would catch a bullet by mean muggin' a muthafucka too long, wake up to bodies stretched across someone's lawn in the hood, or in front of the liquor store a couple of blocks from your child's junior high school. A bloody city where the crime rate is at an all-time high. Where smirky hoes and janky niggas smile in your face, break bread at your table, fuck your bitch, and even your mama while plotting, aiming to snatch the crown. Hell, there can only be one Street King. Vallejo is a place where niggas have no problem putting in that work. You see, me and mine were quick to empty the bulldog when it was time. That's how we get down.... Chasing that chicken, trying to make a quick dollar.

When a nigga is hungry like I am, he's willing to do anything when comes to getting bread, and in a fucked-up situation like getting some real-time thrown at his ass, he'll become selfish, breaking the code, folding like a pile of fresh laundry, quick as fuck. Switching on the niggas he once called his brothers. The true definition of a frenemy.

Nine times out of ten, your niggas ain't your niggas. As you begin to move differently, you start looking at your folks differently also. I was one of these grimy muthafuckas. My ass was young, doing little shit here and there, trying to work my way up in the game. Shit, your boys tell you they love you but how many of them are willing to do that time for you? I wasn't willing to do a day in prison for none of these niggas, and when it came down to it, you come to realize there ain't no love in these streets. Nigga that's rule number one. That's what everyone around me began to realize as I turned. Once I started maneuvering differently, bodies started dropping; bodies of those that I called blood.

I was pulled from my thoughts as 707 by E-40, Nef the Pharaoh, and Willie Joe banged through my car speakers. *I'm throwing up the V....707.... She rolling up the tree....707.... Gotta 223....707.... I'm throwing up the V....707.*

As I mobbed down Benicia Road, going southbound, I couldn't help it as the menacing grin grew across my face because a nigga like me couldn't be touched. I'd just caught my third body in two months, and the boys hadn't come for a nigga yet. Word of me bodying these niggas floated through the town, and I continued to move like I wanted to, doing me. Carmonnie lay slumped with two to the head in the driver's seat of his whip at Wilson Park.

After the boys raided Carmonnie's, where he lived with his moms, the nigga started acting funny. Though he was deeply involved and in the middle of my bullshit, he knew too much. When the nigga started getting nervous on me and questioning my loyalty, I had to dead his ass. I went from trusting my folks to trusting only myself. After I bodied his ass, I hopped in my whip and smashed off, going down Solano Avenue toward Benicia Road. Uno, Dos,

Tres.... My three-day ones were gone and by my hand. Smoke escaped my lips as I bounced to the music. You see, the lives I chose to take, I felt no remorse. Shit, it comes with the territory. I leaned forward and put the half-smoked wood into the ashtray, hitting the gas and turning the slap-up louder in my whip.

Flashing Lights caught my attention, followed by blurp, s and I knew it was the boys. I looked in the rearview mirror and saw these muthafuckas were on my coat tail. The Mac God was chin-checking my ass tonight, fasho, but I wasn't about to give in and go down like that. I hit the gas, forcing the scraper to go as fast as it could. I was in a panic, hitting corners as I sped through hoods and smashed through red lights. Before I knew it, I lost control of the bucket, hitting a telephone pole somewhere on the Hillside of Vallejo. A nigga blacked out, and when I woke up, I was handcuffed to a hospital bed accompanied by two of Vallejo's finest, damn. I tried to lift my head as it ached.

Pressure ran to my forehead as one of the men spoke.

I wouldn't do that if I were you. You fucked your head up running from us and almost hit two people in a crosswalk, he said.

"Man.... Fuck you.", I said and began to cough.

They both chuckled.

"Where you're headed, I'm sure you will get fucked every day."

"No requests needed.", the other officer said.

I didn't say shit else because I knew I was fucked. This was just the beginning. It's over for me. My name is Murk and you're about to read the events of my loyalty, leading to my betrayal.

The Country Club Crest
Chardonnay

"Look, you crazy bitch, I'm done fucking with your weird ass," Jaylon screamed.

"You don't get to walk away from your family.... Jaylon," I fussed.

"You need to chalk this shit up as a loss. You ain't the bitch for me. Yo ass is crazy and psychotic. I love my wife bitch. A nigga like me don't want a psychotic hoe on his arm... I'm back with the wife, and that's what it is. Stay the fuck off my line," Jaylon said.

"We ain't muthafuckin' done. Nigga, I will plant you and that bitch before I let this shit ride. You know how I get down, or do I need to remind you?" I asked.

"Bitch, stay off my nuts though; we done," Jaylon replied.

"Nigga, we ain't done until I say we done," I yelled back into my black and chrome Galaxy S22 before ending the call.

The audacity of this nigga. I believed every lie he spat from his mildew mouth, and my dumb ass fell for the weak shit. I carried this nigga's baby inside me, went hard in the paint for his ass, making sure this nigga was good, pockets stayed thick and all, but the muthafucka still ran back to his punk ass wife. Now I'm sitting here, feeling hella crunchy, but I got something for this hoe-ass nigga. I spun around in the black leather, metal, and gold barstool chair that I sat in and threw my cell across the kitchen, through the doorway entrance that led into the family room. I heard a crack and some glass shatter but didn't give a shit right now.

"Fuck that phone," I thought to myself.

I faced the bottle of E-40's El Cuarenta that sat on the black and gray marble countertop. I drank the bottle halfway down and continued to put a dent in it. The lights in the kitchen were turned down, giving the entire room a warm, yellow glow. As I stared at the bottle of tequila, I began to weep from embarrassment. The hot tears stung as they trickled down my face. I snatched the bottle and brought it to my lips. Who needed a shot glass when they felt like this? I didn't, fasho. Shit, now I know what it feels like to be the second bitch.

"This dirty, janky ass nigga did me foul as fuck....me though?" I questioned myself.

That's when I heard my name echo across the room, directly behind me, along with heavy footsteps. I turned around to face Malay's boyfriend, Murk. Malay was my only daughter. She was only sixteen and in love with this little nigga, but truth is, he was in love with me, and it was kept a secret. After Jaylon pulled his bullshit and ran back to his hoe bitch, nights became lonely, and that's where Murk came in. When Malay wasn't around Murk stayed

pushing up on me. After a while, I became curious and had to see what it did.

"Don't tell me you're here crying behind that cat Jaylon again, Chardonnay," Murk said.

"Just crying behind life period," I answered

"All you gotta do is say the word, and it's on-site," He replied.

"I already know Murk. Always ready to go yanky," I answered.

"Always, and for you, I'll do whatever," he responded.

Yeah, buddy! That's when it dawned on me. Murk was ready for whatever as usual and I needed him to help me handle this fucked up situation that I was in. This nigga talked a boatload of shit and was ready for whatever...whenever. What I do know, the young nigga's name lightweight floated in the streets, and he was ready to put in some real work, some big work. If he wanted it, I had it for him. The way Murk acted told me he gave no fucks, and a nigga that gave no fucks knew no better and didn't mind doing anything to get his hands dirty.

Murk was a tall, brown, and handsome young nigga. His front bottom teeth were slightly crooked, and it was sexy giving him a rugged-ass look. This shit lightweight turned me on. His skin was cocoa brown, his eyes were almond-shaped matching his skin, and his fade held waves so deep that you would get seasick if you stared at them too long.

As Murk stood in front of me, he looked down at me as I looked up at him with our eyes locked on each other. Did I feel bad betraying my daughter as I did? Of course, but I had needs too. Murk was just something to play with and take my mind off Jaylon until he came to his senses.

Murk lifted his hands, wiping the tears from my cheeks as they still fell from my eyes. His hand slowly moved down to my nipple that poked through my blue, spandex tank top. I thought about grabbing his hand to stop the shenanigans but closed my eyes, accepting his touch. My back leaned against the counter with my elbows resting on it. Murk placed soft kisses on my neck while his hand slid down inside my black, cotton boy shorts. I opened my legs, welcoming him.

"Nigga, you just won't let up, will you? You know what we are doing is wrong, and I know it too," I panted as his finger slowly swirled my clit.

Quit fronting, acting like you don't want a nigga and shit. Lay at a party in the crest and won't be back no time soon. So, what's up? I got what you need to take your mind off that square anyway. You know that shit already though. Murk whispered in my ear as he continued to play with my pussy.

Fuck it. I am human and have needs just like the next bitch. I wrapped my arms around Murk, and he lifted me off the chair, sitting me on the countertop, and slowly pulled down my shorts, tossing them across the room. He sat on the chair in front of me and dove in my pussy. I lifted my legs over his shoulders as he slurped down my juices and tickled my clit.

"Damn, nigga, I cried as my nut started to rise.

My ass rocked back and forth, and my hips circled with each stroke that he gave me as he sent shivery chills through my body.

Murk baby, don't stop, I yelped, and I came in his mouth. Murk lifted me off the counter and carried me to the bedroom. Lil' daddy had a long dick for days, and I needed that shit. After I got served, we had some shit to chop up. I was about to dead this bitch and this bitch ass nigga.

Jaylon was a dumb ass nigga to think he could work me and sit me on the shelf like a used toy ready to collect dust when he was done with my ass. The nigga had me fucked up if he thought I was going to raise Shalia alone because he woke up one day and decided he didn't want to play daddy anymore. This nigga had me and the game fucked up. I was the wrong bitch to fuck with, and I thought he knew that. It was time for Chardonnay to know what it felt like to catch a couple of bodies.

When it came to Murk, there was nothing but physical attraction. There were no feelings attached. I had the lil' nigga right where I wanted him, in the palm of my hand. Why not give his ass some of this grown-ass pussy and make him lose his mind even more so he would do whatever I asked? If he came through for me, Murk could have this pussy whenever he wanted.

30 minutes later

Our bodies dripped from sweat as we lay naked next to each other while we both panted, catching our breath.

"So, what's up, Chardonnay? You want to tell me about that shit in the kitchen," Murk asked.

Tears filled my eyes as I tried to fight them back. I was tired of crying over Jaylon. It was time he felt me in a major way.

"Jaylon is still with the shits. I keep trying to get that nigga to come around," I said.

"Are you going to continue to cry or handle the situation," Murk asked.

"Get dressed, and let's take a right. I need to holla at you about something," I said.

Like I said before, I had Murk right where I wanted him. It was time for me to feel a little satisfaction for a change instead of being stepped on all the damn time. He would be my little puppet until I was done with him and ready to sit his ass on the shelf to collect damn dust.

The Next Night
Murk

I knew Chardonnay would give in and let a nigga beat on her walls again after I licked on her pussy real good. I knew her pretty ass was lightweight feeling a nigga. Jaylon treated her like shit and left her ass in the dust when he got tired of her. Lay wasn't giving up the pussy, and I stayed with her ass just to be close to Chardonnay.

The shit worked out cool for me.

I usually got what I wanted even if I had to take it.... from whoever, sparing no feeling when it came to me getting mine. I rocked with quite a few niggas, but Carmonni, Skitzo, and Danelli were my solid niggas who I called my brothers. They were niggas I could trust, my main dogs. We worked the streets ganking niggas selling what we could, trying to get what we thought was ours, you know, busting moves getting that cheese.

Chardonnay spit to me last night about her and Jaylon's bullshit, complaining about how he left her for the wife.

Some shit I already knew, but what I didn't know, her veins had ice in them like mine, and when she started talking big money and telling me she wanted this nigga and his bitch bodied, it made me want her ass even more. My baby had all of my attention when she mentioned the bread though. When it came to chicken, my dick always got hard.

Ole girl promised me twenty-five racks if I came through for her. This would be a big move for me. One that I've been waiting for, but I was going to need one of my niggas with me on this one. I needed to holla at Danelli so we could get this bread. This nigga was a young hog in the making like me, and we've been rocking since the womb.

Cuddy is always ready to get in anytime.... anywhere. I wasn't about to pass this proposition up for a damn thang.

Me and Chardonnay hopped in her black 2022 Jaguar F-Pace that had the black leather seats, taking a ride last night. We drove to the

South-side and parked on the corner of Grant Street. Jaylon's tilt was on the next block and

Chardonnay didn't want her truck to be seen. When we approached Jaylon's spot, the lights were dim inside the house... We stood in the yard next to an oak tree, staring through the window. The burgundy, sheer drapes were gaped open, and we watched as Jaylon and his wife sat cuddled on the black leather sectional as they watched a movie.

"So, this the tilt huh?" I asked.

"Yeah, this they spot," She replied, still looking past the drapes that flowed with the wind.

I watched closely as Chardonnay's nostrils flared open, and her cheeks began to turn beet red. She bit down on her full bottom lip, cringing at what she saw. This nigga chose u, and now there would be consequences.

"Check this out though. Me and my boy will slide through here for the next couple of weeks and peep shit, seeing how these muthafuckas move and plan this shit out carefully. Afterward, I'll let you know when it's time to make some noise. If you're cool with it and give us the green light, it's a go," I said.

"Aight, lil' daddy. Don't let me down," she said as she turned in my direction.

Chardonnay stood there, glaring at me with those dark eyes, but the stare was blank and cold. It was the first time I'd seen her look this way.

"Look, make sure this is what you want to do because once it's done, it's done. Ain't no going back," I said.

"Ain't shit to think about. Let's go before somebody sees us," she said dry as fuck, walking back to the car.

We barely spoke in the car on the way to Chardonnay's tilt. Her ass was butt-ass hurt at what she saw. I chose not to say shit. The last thing I wanted was my baby getting mad at me and changing her mind.

I wasn't about to fuck this up. I sat back and let soak in the shit she'd seen tonight. Once I was back to my car, I dipped. Malay called a few times, but I wasn't fucking with her right now. I had some real nigga shit to handle, so she was on the back burner for now.

"Vallejo...Bitch!" Banged in my ears.

As soon as I heard those two words blast through my speakers, I turned up the slap.

"Yeah, best of the best. Old school central, new school west. Driveway boy, I can say it with my chest, and I rep spit corner till my very last breath. Like a five-nine fifth, flamed up C-cap. Stick to the strip-like dreads through the beeswax. Haaaaa.... Let's get this clear. Yawl cats just visit; y'all don't live out here."

As I moved through the streets of the V, I pulled out my cell and sent Danelli a text to see where this nigga was posted. I was about to slide through and put this bug in his ear about this hustle and getting this bread.

Once I chopped it up with the nigga, letting him know what it was and who, his ass was with it.

"Cuddy, what we waiting on?" Dannelli asked.

"Be cool, nigga. Yo ass ready to go make fireworks already," I answered.

"What the fuck we need to wait for? We already know what we need to do. Body the bitch and rock that nigga shit. So, what the fuck we standing around here debating about it for?" He questioned me.

"Look, blood, we don't want to get caught up. These muthafuckas could have hammers all over the house.

Let's just do our homework for the next two weeks, peep how they move, see who they fuck with and who they know. Nigga, you know what I'm talking about. When Chardonnay says it's time, then we can make it sound like the Fourth of July...Aight?" I spoke and questioned...

"Yeah nigga, aight. You know I stay with the shits, ready for whatever. Can you trust ole girl, though?" Danelli asked.

"Nigga, she good, and we go be good after we handle this shit," I said.

"Ok....Ok. You, my brother, and I trust you. If you say she is straight, then it's on. We are about to do this shit," he said, dapping me down.

Over the next two weeks, we peeped the game, seeing who came in and out of the tilt. There could be no fuck ups, or it was a wrap for everybody.

Chapter Two

Millersville

Danelli

I was slightly irritated, watching muthafuckas eating dinner and having movie nights, cupcakes up on the couch all night. This was some weak shit. I was ready to handle this shit and get the bread. I knew we had to play right without getting caught up, but damn, this shit was moving too slow. A nigga like me never played by the rules when it came to the streets. Shit, none of the niggas I knew, never did. We dipped after a text came through from this lil' bitch, Fadrah. She lived in the Ville off Star Avenue.

"Say nigga, drop me off at Franklin Middle school," I said.

"What you getting into?" Murk asked.

"Trying to see what this little bitch Fadrah is willing to do for a nigga tonight, ole girl been stretching her neck out," I said as I text her, letting her know I'm getting dropped off.

Look nigga; word is that bitch aint cool. Yeah, she on some hoe shit, but what I got a problem with is the bitch coming around our people but be around our enemies too. You know that ain't cool. A bitch like that, you better watch," Murk replied.

"Well, she's about to watch this dick tonight, nigga," I joked.

"Man.... you better watch that hoe. I'm just saying," Murk said.

"I feel you, bro. Good looking out though," I said.

"You got a hammer on you?" He asked me.

"At all times, nigga. You know how I roll," I replied.

"Aight. Holla at me when you get back to the tilt," Murk said.

"Fasho, Brodie," I said and hopped out the whip.

Murk skirted off, and I decided to cut through the back of the school instead of walking the streets. It was dark as shit too. I walked through the parking lot, past the office, around the left side of the school building, passing a few bushes and a couple of trees. As I approached the back of the building, I heard movement. It sounded like shoes scuffling behind me. As I continued to walk, I reached down my pants, pulled out the hammer, and turned around with my thumper aimed and ready,

"What's up nigga? I knew we would see each other again. I said as I focused on this hoe-ass nigga Ladario from College Park.

I put two in the niggas chest before he could make any sudden moves. He fell and landed on his back. Now, I'm wondering how this nigga happened to creep upon my ass out of the blue. I walked over to his ass with my hammer still pointed at him.

"Nigga, you ain't that smart to know where I would be. How you find me?" I asked.

Ladario tried to speak but choked on the blood he was coughing up. Me and Ladario used to be cool until he started robbing all the lil' niggas we fucked with. Going around Vallejo, wearing a ski mask, robbing his own people on some janky shit. Once word began floating around the town, it was him. Ladario started moving in silence and ducking off where nobody could find his ass. The streets were talking, and this nigga was M.I.A. I heard he started gaffing niggas all over the Bay Area. Where he really fucked up, was kicking my mom's door in while I wasn't home and robbing me for my shit that I had stashed. The bitch tore mom's house up, searching until he found what he was looking for. You see, all of us niggas grew up together, and we all met on the school bus that moms drove. We were solid, but as we got older, we found out who our real niggas were, and sometimes it to us a little longer to see who our true enemies were.

When Ladario came to rob me, I was nowhere to be found. Mom was home alone, and this nigga wore his ski mask, but when he spoke asking where the money was at, mom recognized the niggas voice, and when she busted his ass out, he went too far, pistol-whipped her and all. For that, he had to take a dirt nap. It was the only way.

Music started going off, and it was coming from his pocket. Vallejo Nigga by Mac Duna and E40 was playing.

I'm from the V the Valley J.... Vallejo Nigga. We with the fist and pistol play.... Vallejo nigga.

I squatted down, reaching in the niggas black Canada Goose puffer jacket that had two holes in the front right side from my hammer. I pulled the silver Apple iPhone 13 Pro Max from his pocket and looked to see who was calling this nigga.

"Nigga, say it ain't so. Fadrah tried to set a nigga up, huh? Ima hold on to this for you, potna," I said.

I tucked the thumper back in my pants and pulled my cell out and called Murk.

"Damn nigga, Fadrah done with yo ass already," he asked as he laughed into the phone.

"Nigga, bust a bitch and come snatch my ass up real quick. I'll be up the way at the liquor store," I said.

"On my way," he said, ending the call.

Fadrah pulled my hoe card tonight, and for that, she had to get her back dirty. I can't get caught slipping behind a hoe bitch or some muthafuckin' pussy. Mom's always talking about bitches like that, but I never listened, and tonight the shit almost got me bodied. I should've paid more attention when Mom was lacing me with game about these nothing-ass hoes.

I ran back to the front of the school. The liquor store was a few blocks away. When I made it there, Murk was already parked, waiting on my ass.

I hopped in the whip. Gasping, trying to catch my breath from fleeing the scene. Sweat dripped from my face, and my skin was cold and clammy under the black, leather, down-filled Tom Ford jacket that I wore. As Murk smashed off, bypassing the school we heard police sirens in the distance grow, becoming louder, coming in our direction until we saw them speed past us.

"Blood, I was gone for two minutes. What went down?" Murk asked.

"Fadrah tried to set a nigga up," I answered.

"I tried to warn you nigga. What you do to her," he asked.

"Nigga, nothing yet, but guess who tried to run up on me like he was gonna catch me slipping though," I asked.

"Who, bro, who?" Murk was curious to know.

"That sucka Ladario. I popped his ass twice in the chest. As soon as I did, Fadrah started calling the nigga phone. Probably heard the shots and thought the nigga got my ass, but I'm coming for that bitch," I said.

"Damn nigga, she a foul bitch for that, but I told you," Murk said.

"Drop me off at the tilt. Ima take care of that hoe. Fadrah ain't gotta clue that I know. I want to keep it that way until I catch her slipping," I said.

No doubt, I was going to find some shit in that phone that had to do with everything that happened tonight. I knew a few bitches that were on some nigga shit, too, and would handle this hoe. What I was planning for this bitch would be unforgettable. I was going to make sure she remembered my ass.

The Country Club Crest
Chardonnay

I had the spot all to myself for the weekend. My mother took the Shalia and Malay was at her friend's until Sunday night. I couldn't get over the sight of Jaylon and his wife and how I was on the outside looking in. The image played over and over in my head, sending me into a frantic rage as I repeatedly dwelled on the shit. No matter how hard I tried to shake the thought from my head, the image of the two remained there.... Stuck as fuck in my head.

I was spoiled and an only child. I got whatever I wanted and can't remember a time when my mother told me no. It was the first time I didn't get what I wanted, and the first time I knew what it felt like to lose. Fuck chalking this shit up to the game. Jaylon made it clear that I was cut off, and he didn't want to have anything to do with me or his child. He didn't want me anymore, but I wanted him, and if I couldn't have him, then I wanted him.... Dead.

Malay's father was an older man who had long money. He was my cat daddy, and though the relationship didn't last long when he passed away, he made sure I was taken care of. He'd never been married and had no other family, so once he was gone, everything was left to me and my daughter. I enjoyed living the single life until Jaylon came along and disrupted my peace. If the nigga would've left me the fuck alone, we wouldn't be in this fucked up space we're in today.

Fresh out of the shower, oiled up, and smelling right, I stood in front of the bathroom mirror, thinking about what Murk said, making sure that I wanted to go through with this. I didn't have to think long. My mind was made up, and there would be no regrets on my end. I've waited long enough, and it was time to serve this nigga some get right. I stood in front of the bathroom mirror as I did my makeup. Murk called me after he found out that Malay was gone for the weekend. His ass would pop up on my ass out of the blue as he usually did. I got sexy as

I waited for him to come through. I need to fuck his ass one more time to keep him satisfied so that he would follow suit and do as I asked.

After my make-up was done, I walked into the bedroom to get dressed. I had 30 minutes before the nigga would be here. Laid upon my bed was my red Hollywood Dream Sweetheart corset from Fredricks that was trimmed with lightly boned lining along with the panties that matched. Once I was dressed, I turned around to face the mirror, admiring the Jacquard and Venice lace trim that was around my neckline, and I loved how the corset gave my body an hourglass look.

I smirked as I stared at myself in the mirror, thinking to myself, if I could, I would fuck me too.

My brown, shoulder-length hair held naturally loose girls. I decided to wear it pinned up, leaving out a few strands around my edges to show off my neckline. I walked over to the walk-in closet and grabbed my red Loubi Queen Alta's that had the stiletto heel along with the ankle strap. Shit, I was going to need a few shots before Murk got here, so I strutted my cute ass into the kitchen. The sound of my heels tapping the hardwood floor as I walked into the kitchen echoed throughout the quiet house.

It was a Henn type of night for me and that's what I decided to drink. I was pouring my third shot when I heard the loud ass music from someone's car as they pulled in front of the tilt. It was nobody but Murk's ass. It was time to give his young ass some pussy.

Tonight, I was going to let this nigga have his way, doing whatever he wanted to me as I submitted to him.

Once this business transaction we have is finished, so are we. I thought about Murk riding off into the sunset with my ass, but we could never be, and I didn't want to crush Malay's heart. I've been thinking about relocating, maybe out of state. I don't want any parts of the aftermath when this shit goes left. I decided to meet up with some of my partners tomorrow night while Murk did his thang. That way, when this shit gets funky, I'll have my alibi. I want as many people as possible to see my face when I hit the streets tomorrow night...

Three Hours later

I was positioned on my stomach, stretched across my bed, fully naked, panting, and ready to tap out for the night. Murk went in, banging on my pussy walls like some African drums. I tried tapping out thirty minutes into our session, but the nigga wasn't having it. His grip was strong as fuck as he continued to slide in and out of me until his gas ran out. The dick was A-1, and he knew how to apply pressure and knew how to serve a bitch well.

"Are you ready to handle that?" I asked.

"I stay ready. Fuck kind of question is that? I was just waiting on that green light, Chardonnay. The question is, are you ready? Once it's done, ain't no undoing it," Murk said as he stood in the doorway watching me.

"Nigga, I know that. So, what's up with tomorrow night; is that cool?" I asked.

"It's good. I'll hit up my folks and let them know. After we handle this shit, I'll hit your line and see where you want to meet up," He answered.

"That's cool," I answered.

The room became quiet, and my tipsy ass passed out. When I woke up the next morning, Murk was gone.

This nigga better come through as he promised, or I was cutting his fucking water off sooner.

My plans for today were to meet up with some of my real bitches tonight, paint the town, and hit a few bars while Murk did his thang. I need all of the V to see my face tonight in case I need an alibi. He could get caught up for this shit, but my ass refused to take a loss like that.

West Vallejo
Run Me My Fade
Danelli

This Sheisty bitch Farah was on slick snake shit like I thought. She tried to set a nigga up, but when I see this hoe, it's on sight.... Straight like that. She was going to catch a muthafucking fade. I was linking up with Murk later to do the damn thang but not before sliding through my OG potna Guap's tilt.

He was having a party for his baby moms, and I decided to slide through and holla at the big homie.

When I walked into the spot, the music was banging with a whole lot of asses moving. *S.O.B AND R.B.E, Bitch, I'm The Boy, Who the Fuck*, quaked through the tilt, rattling windows, and vibrating frames. *Day ones only I don't really fuck with new niggas, Choppa like a thot, touch one you'll get blue nigga. Gangin Gangin bitch I be gangin. Choppa start sanging if yo mouth where my name is.*

The disco ball lightweight had a nigga head spinning along with the LV pill I'd popped 30 minutes ago. The twins had hit my line earlier, letting me know they spotted this bitch at the party. I dapped a couple of niggas down and kept it moving after I walked in the tilt. I found a corner to post up with my hoodie on my head. As I bopped my head to the music, I threw L's up, giving the twins the green light if they saw me. Screams and yells broke out over the music, and I walked over, watching the twins as they both rocked Farah's shit. She looked confused until I pulled the hoodie off of my head so she could see me. I grabbed the twins' arms and stepped in.

"Since you on some set, a nigga up shit, run me my muthafuckin' fade. You about to get ya back dirty.... Snake bitch. Now tear this bitch shit up," I said to the twins and walked away.

The Su-side
Murk

After the party, me and Danelli smashed from the West Side of the V to the south. Hammers lay on our lap as the car floated through the green lights while we dipped through Sonoma Blvd. There wasn't much talking because I had my music up, beating through the speakers. Raining game by Mac Dre had us feeling ourselves as we bopped our heads to the music.

Hop out of the shower, turn on the beat, and start to jamming. Put on my Pelle Pelle shirt made by Mark Buchanan. I'm slamming Suga Wolf cuz he is a straight hog. Put on my Abercrombie coat to cope with the bay fog.

I stay sharp, my job is peeling them top notches. I got bitches, and Mac driggidy stayed cautious. Gotta watch the yermi movie cuz, man, I got to warn ya, it's a rainy game in Northern California. I'm extra flossy and saucy, so I pop collars and clock dollars.... We got that sauce like boss players, we floss the cleaners, push the Dayton, and some of us roll on ninas. Straight lace, triple gold, it's difficult not to jock, she's looking famous, so you know that I got to knock. Gotta peep the scene though, cuz with these hoes, you might get played by one of them hoes wearing weaves, bobs, or braids.

The scraper slowed down as I hit the brakes, as I passed the M&M liquor store on Sonoma, turned left on the Lemon tree, pulling in front of the park across the street from Lemon Tree Trailor Park. We already knew what to do.

Get in, handle it, and get out. There was no point in speaking on it again.

This spot where we parked was straight. It was dark, and there were no streetlights. Moving in the dark was best. At night the park was empty, and a nigga was trying to be seen. I turned the car off, pulled the keys from the ignition, and grabbed the hammer from my lap, tucking it in the back of my paints.

"Let's do this shit nigga", I said.

Fasho, fasho. Danelli responded.

We walked a couple of blocks up and hit a left, passing M&Ms, the neighborhood liquor store. A few minutes later, we stand in front of Jaylon's tilt, pulling down our ski masks. I followed Danelli as he went two steps up, checking the door. He twists the doorknob, and it's locked.

He looks back at me and shakes his head. I wave my hand and point to the side of the house. He follows me to the sliding door. The second time and we had luck. The Mack God was on our side tonight...

We walked in, guns aimed, walking to the living room where I knew Jaylon and his wife were usually posted.

"Yeah, nigga! What it do?" I yelled.

"What the fuck is this?" Jaylon asked as he jumped up.

I hit this nigga with the butt of the hammer, and he fell back on the couch next to his wife, who was screaming.

"Aye bitch shut the fuck up! Cuddy, he moves again, give his ass the business," I said.

His wife's screams echoed through the house as they grew louder. Shit was irritating the fuck out of me. I just felt the need to shut the bitch up. I popped one into her chest, and her cries for help turned into begging gurgles for breath

Jaylon leaped forward, and Danelli's finger trigger got loose.

"Compliments of Chardonnay," I said as I watched Jaylon's body go limp.

"Let's dip," Danelli said.

Suddenly sirens and blurps growled in the distance, growing closer as each second passed. We knew they were coming our way, and we fled the scene. When we hit Lemon Tree approaching the whip, I looked up the hill on Solano and saw flashes as the boys swarmed the neighborhood. We jumped in the car, barely escaping.

"Cuddy, that's two bodies in one night," Danelli said.

"We bout that life nigga, and if we don't get that bread we owed, it's about to be three bodies," I responded.

I knew we had to duck off somewhere, but not until Chardonnay paid in full. She owed a nigga some chicken, and I was coming for it. I was going to hit her ass up tonight. I did my part, and now she had to do hers and she would want to think before trying to fuck me over. If she could turn ice cold on her baby daddy, she would do it to me too.

My Office
Chardonnay

I was too turn't tonight, perkin' like a muthafucka, and feeling myself. My office was the third bar we hit up tonight, and all eyes were on me. I had on my thigh, Bailey boyfriend, ankle, blue jeans, and my black Louis Vuitton Laureate boots with the top to match. I stayed with the drip but ready to drag a hoe no matter where I went. I stayed trying to be seen, all bullshit to the side. You could say I wanted to be famous. I stepped into the bar looking fly, but I usually did when I step out, being seen by all of Vallejo. I wiggled my hips and juggled my ass as B-legits Money over the bullshit slapped through the building.

My lil' nigga asked me about Illuminati, I told him, God over everybody. I'm in the party, with the white Louis on the floor, in the Sac with my mac, blowing dough. Yo, everybody knows in Mexico, you get em' for the low, then you get em out the doe. Back to the state, everythang looking great, by the morning, I can make about a million eight. Yeah, I sleep late when I'm in the land, hard head nigga, never could understand. AP about a hundred grand, they get across, and I'm coming with the contraband. I get 'em' off on the count soft, stack racks, how else Ima bounce back? Matter of fact, MOB to the enemy.

I mingled through the night. There were niggas I hadn't seen in a while, and they paid for my cocktails, but I went home alone at the end of the night. After leaving the bar, it was a wrap; It was three in the morning, and everything was closed. I pulled my cell out of my reversible tan and white Louis Vuitton tote to see that Murk called hella times.

"Shit. I need to call this nigga back," I said aloud.

I decided to text him instead. It was late, and I was too turnt and needed to sleep that shit off.

Murk. Just saw your missed calls. Call you in the A.M, boo.

When I pulled to my spot, I walked across my grass, up the porch, and unlocked my front door. I had too much to drink and passed out in the clothes I wore as soon as my ass touched the bed. When I woke up the next day I sat at my countertop and ate my breakfast. A bowl of mixed berries, as usual, along with a glass of orange juice. I took a sip of my juice as I saw the words across the bottom of my television screen. Vallejo man and woman shot, one dead one in critical condition. My ass almost choked. I ran to my room, grabbed my cell off of the nightstand, and called Murk. He answered on the first ring.

"What the fuck, Chardonnay! I've been calling you all night. How you leave a nigga hanging like that?" He fussed in my ear.

"That's my bad, Murk. I passed out drunk last night," I answered.

We need to meet up and handle that transaction as promised.

"You fucked up Murk, one still breathing," I said

"Chardonnay don't fuck with me," I said.

"Finish the job, and don't call me back until it's done, nigga." I said and ended the call.

Murk was calling for money and pussy, but until ole boy finishes what I asked, he gets nada. When I told him to come through and put in this work, that's what I expected; nothing less. Until there were two bodies, he was asked out. The nigga was stuck as fuck until he came through like I asked.

Fuck Em' and Feed Em' Fish

Murk

"Nigga.... fuck you mean. That bitch burnt us. She needs to run me mine.... straight up!" Danelli fussed.

"Cuddy, when I get paid, you get paid. She says one of em' still breathing. They come out of this, we fucked, dude, but it's impossible to just walk in the hospital and finish what we started." I said.

"Nigga this ain't cool...so now what? We out here taking penitentiary chances on g-p.... huh?"

"I got this bitch, but until then, we need to tuck off somewhere, and hide out for a while."

Me and Danelli decided to separate and post up somewhere. This shit became sloppy, and instead of two bodies, there was one, but Chardonnay had me fuck up. I don't give a fuck how fine or how good the pussy was; she was going to run me mine....one me.

Lay was blowing up my fucking line, but she was cut the fuck off. This hubba head Chandra drove me around in her bucket instead of driving my whip. The last thing I needed was the boys running my plates and shit going left.

Threw that hoe some powder, and she was with it. A week had passed as I continued to hit up Chardonnay. The last call I made to her; this hoe changed her number.

"Chandra, drive me to the Crest side and hit Kemper Street," I demanded.

"Aight nigga." She replied.

Rolling through the crest. Niggas was out doing the damn thang as usual at noon. When I hit Kemper, it was dead qs fuck beside the flashing lights coming from three police cars. As we slowly rolled by, I saw Chardonnay being handcuffed and escorted down the steps of the porch by one of Vallejo's finest. All bullshit to the side, I became panicked as fuck. I hope this muthatucka knows how to keep her bridge down.

Three days later, I was arrested while I as was laid up at a bando in Millerville when the boys raided the spot.

When these muthafuckas brought me down to the station, they were throwing 10 plus at my ass. Chardonnay sang like she was the leader of the church choir on a 4th Sunday. This bitch let her lips get loose and t old these punk ass niggas everythang, giving up names and all the shit. The only name she couldn't give up was Danelli's because I never told her.

As she told me, so did I, giving up every name, including Danelli. I was like a bluebird that came around on those early spring mornings, singing as loud as I could. If I could get out of this without doing ten, I would. I gave them Danelli's name and told them how to find the nigga and all. My ass did three weeks, but my boy wound up with the ten. I just wasn't ready to do that time, and Chardonnay was behind a jail cell waiting to go to trial. When I was released, niggas asked questions, and I told lies.

Chardonnay

These little dumb ass niggas fucked off everything. They left Jaylon breathing. As soon as old boy was able to talk to the boys, my name escaped his lips. Instead of deading his ass Murk had to give this nigga my name, letting Jaylon know I sent their ass. This shit went left and quick. I tried to do everything I could to keep my name as far away from this shit as I could and failed. The boys didn't have a clue who did the shooting, but that was about to change. I wasn't going out by myself. Murk was going down with me. He fucked this up. It was his fault I was sitting here, waiting to go to trial facing murder charges and shit.

I didn't know who ole boy was that was with him, but Murk knew. What I didn't think was that he would tell on his own nigga. This nigga was on some canary shit. Murk did seem the type to fold on his niggas, looking out for only himself now that I sit back and think of shit. Damn, I wonder how this shit was going to play out when his boy finds out. Me....I was stuck as fuçk. I'll be in my casket when sunlight shines my way again.

My baby girl will be raised by my mother and Lay on her fucking own. I let my jealousy get the best of me and tear my family apart. Now I'm posted in the county looking stupid as fuck.

Six Years Later
Danelli

This hoe ass nigga did three weeks, got out, and was back on the streets like it was nothing while my ass was stuck, doing six out of ten. At one point, we were brothers, but now we are enemies. I continued to stare at the paper I held in my hand with Murk's confession on it.

When I see him, it's on sight. After I dealt with this nigga everybody around the town would know Murk wasn't shit but a snitch ass nigga, and he can't be trusted. I'll be out this bitch in one more week, but until then, I had to get the paper mailed out to my boy Skitzo and get the muthafucka floating all over Facebook.

I couldn't wait to hear the lies he would try to tell after niggas and bitches questioned. Him about this fucking paper. Square ass nigga had to be checked when I hit the streets again. I folded the paperwork and carefully placed it and the letter I wrote in an envelope. I licked the flap and sealed it and placed it on my desk. I picked up the blue pen and wrote Skito's address on the bottom right and my address on the top left. I knew what it felt like to be betrayed by a brother, and when I see the dude, he had no choice but to run me my muthafucking fade.

As soon as I touched down and this nigga Murk heard, the rat muthafucka had the nerve to hit my line.

"Brodie, why you going around telling niggas I told on you?" Mirk asked.

"Nigga you sang, and for that, you gotta to run me my fade....straight like that," I said and ended the call.

It could be tomorrow or a year from now, but I was going to see this nigga about something. Two weeks passed, and shit was dead. Murk never called my phone again but two weeks later, I saw the nigga.

My ass was posted at the tilt, chilling on the couch watching Power Universe. There was a loud knock on the front door. I stood and walked over to the front door and looked through the screen, seeing it was my nigga, T-money.

"What it do, my nigga." I said as I opened the screen.

"Cuddy take a walk with me and smoke with your boy one time." He said.

"Aight nigga." I replied.

As I walked down Georgia Street a chill came over me. It was spring, no wind blew, and the sun stood out in the clear blue sky. There wasn't much traffic. I shook the chill off and continued to walk.

Moments passed when I saw a blue Toyota Corolla coming toward me. The car slowed down as it approached me and my eyes met Murk.

"Get out the car nigga and run me my fade!" I yelled.

I don't know who the lil nigga was that was behind the driver's side, but he can get it too. Murk smirked and the car sped up and hit the block coming around again. This time when the car approached me bullet flew, and I was hit in the neck, chest, and side. Blood filled my mouth as I gasped for air. Tires screeched, and the whip burned rubber and people off. I fell to the ground and moments later I was dead.

BAY BIZZNESS

Murk

I had my young nigga Carmonni take his mom's car while she was at work and hit up T-money. I paid his ass to get Danelli out of the house for this little setup. We used to be like blood, inseparable, fucking family, but those days were over.

I knew I'd bodied the nigga after the lead hit his neck and he struggled to breathe but I didn't wait around for the boys to come. Carmonni smashed back to his mom's and parked the car in the garage. We went inside and hid the hammer in a wall heater inside his mother's living room. I scroll Facebook and Instagram hoping I would hear some shit. Around five that afternoon photos of Danelli flooded both timeliness along with RIP. The cold part about it. I felt no remorse and was ready to body D-Boy.

D-boy let me post up at his tilt even though he heard it was me that bodied Danelli. I was there about a month and decided to rob the nigga for all of his shit when he was gone. He called and called, hitting my line until I answered two weeks later, telling him to let squash this beef and to meet me at Blue Rock Springs Park. He was with. The nigga called early the next morning around 6 AM and I hopped in my whip to go meet him with a choppa on my lap. When I pulled into the parking lot, D-Boy was sitting in front of one of the park benches.

I learned my lesson about talking too much. I lifted the choppa and let em' fly as I drove past the nigga. His body became slumped and tilted to the side as blood seeped from his chest. Three weeks later, I bodied Carmonnie. As I said before...Uno, dos, Tres. Three of my brothers are gone and by my hand.

Murk

I had my young nigga Carmonni take his mom's car while she was at work and hit up T-money. I paid his ass to get Danelli out of the house for this little setup. We used to be like blood, inseparable, fucking family, but those days were over.

I knew I'd bodied the nigga after the lead hit his neck and he struggled to breathe but I didn't wait around for the boys to come. Carmonni smashed back to his mom's and parked the car in the garage. We went inside and hid the hammer in a wall heater inside his mother's living room. I scroll Facebook and Instagram hoping I would hear some shit. Around five that afternoon photos of Danelli flooded both timeliness along with RIP. The cold part about it. I felt no remorse and was ready to body D-Boy.

D-boy let me post up at his tilt even though he heard it was me that bodied Danelli. I was there about a month and decided to rob the nigga for all of his shit when he was gone. He called and called, hitting my line until I answered two weeks later, telling him to let squash this beef and to meet me at Blue Rock Springs Park. He was with. The nigga called early the next morning around 6 AM and I hopped in my whip to go meet him with a choppa on my lap. When I pulled into the parking lot, D-Boy was sitting in front of one of the park benches.

I learned my lesson about talking too much. I lifted the choppa and let em' fly as I drove past the nigga. His body became slumped and tilted to the side as blood seeped from his chest. Three weeks later, I bodied Carmonnie. As I said before...Uno, dos, Tres. Three of my brothers are gone and by my hand.

Solano County Jail

Chardonnay

It's been six long fucking years behind these fucked up walls. Every day that I'm in this place I fight for two things.... my life and my freedom. Nights that I lay awake, I think about the fucked-up shit I've done. Not only did I embarrass and ruin my children's lives, but I ruined the lives of other families also. Some of their mothers will never be able to hug and hear their son's voices again. The only thing they can do is visit them at their graves. For that I know I'm going to hell with gasoline draws on.... first class.

I fell in love and had a child with a married man who didn't love me back. Instead of letting go, I tried to hold on to some shit that was never there. As I finish out my twenty-five-year sentence Jaylon and his wife happily grow old together, making the family that I wanted.

I've done some dirty shit, wondering if I were out would I still be manipulative and evil as I've been? I'm sure I would. I was a spoiled bitch, and I could help but to want more. How could I have stooped so low, sleeping with my daughter's boyfriend, and wanting the father of my child dead? I felt like shit ever since the day of my arrest.

This is my first time in prison and realizing that a pretty bitch like me wasn't built for this shit. All of the dark shit and guilt stay in my head, but it will be over soon. I stood in front of the cell door, waiting for it to open. I closed my eyes and tears fell as I hear the latch and the metal doors opening for my ass to go to breakfast but this morning my plans were different. As soon as the door opened, I ran, leaping over the side rail, and falling down five flights.

The last thing I remember is a loud crack and sharp pain in my head before it split open.

Murk

I believed every word that Chardonnay let creep from her lying lips. I should've paid attention to every little detail, paid attention to this snake bitch as she played me until it was game over. That's what happens when you get thrown off behind a piece of good ass. By the time I realized who the fuck Chardonnay was and what she stood for, it was too late.

I learned firsthand that the power of the pussy can get you caught up, make you switch up, and do other shit out of character even when it's not yours. Jaylon's name was stamped all over Chardonnay from head to toe, but I was young, dumb, and too damn blind to see the truth for what it really was. One of the rules I forgot to abide by, don't trust these hoes. I let this bitch's fine looks and good pussy mesmerize me and take control of my mind.

I folded, turning on my brothers and making their mothers cry from the grief of losing a child. I wanted to be the man and respected in the streets, moving about it the wrong way. My head became too big, making me feel as if I could be touched.

I went from rocking with my brothers to turning on the niggas because of greed, jealousy, and my reputation being exposed. I often ask myself if I feel guilty for the shit I've done, and I don't. The only thing I feel guilty about is getting caught. What I did realize is I can be touched like anyone else. I have all the time in the world to think about the shit as I sit in Solano County Jail, waiting to be tried as a serial murderer. That's fucked up because I had one more body to catch.

The End...Or is it?

About The Publisher

A Hear That Ink LLC Audiobook Production in association with Dean Hamid LLC.

This book is exclusively available as a audiobook @ www.hearthatink.com[1]

Also available from Hear That Ink LLC Audiobook Production:

Five Tales from Gotham

Lost Boy

Epidemic 7.3k

And, a large assortment of free audiobooks as well.

Hear That Ink LLC Audiobook Production

"...for all your audiobook needs."

---

1.   http://www.hearthatink.com

About the Author

Lyrics Brown. San Francisco, home to plenty duplicated by many. Diversity, Originality, Charisma, the Sucka Free has it all. Forever in the battle, win, lose or draw.

Christina Bradshaw known as Author Caleigh Blue writes Fiction Romance based out of the bay area. She has four children and eight grandchildren.

My name is Author Khatari aka Author De'Kari. I write under two pen names and have a total of 16 books published, 17 with this anthology. I love to write books and poetry, fishing, sports and mentoring youth.

A Pittsburg, CA native, Danae Braggs is an all-around SUPER WOMAN. She soared above the odds and surpassed lackluster expectations. Today she is a successful entrepreneur, real estate agent, and author; just to name a few of her many accomplishments.